W9-BMO-077

WRESTLING
WITH HONOR

WRESTLING
WITH HONOR

DAVID KLASS

LODESTAR BOOKS
E. P. Dutton   New York

Copyright © 1989 by David Klass

Library of Congress Cataloging-in-Publication Data

Klass, David.
   Wrestling with honor / by David Klass.—1st ed.
     p. cm.
   "Lodestar books."
   Summary: Champion high school wrestler Ron Woods faces a soul-searching season when he refuses to retake a mandatory drug test he has failed. The decision affects every area of his life, including his feelings about his father, who died in Vietnam, and his first tentative romance.
   ISBN 0-525-67268-0
   [1. Wrestling—Fiction. 2. Drug testing—Fiction. 3. Conduct of life—Fiction. 4. Interpersonal relations—Fiction. 5. Fathers and sons—Fiction.]
I. Title.   88-16147
PZ7.K67813Wr   1988   CIP
[Fic]—dc19   AC

Published in the United States by Lodestar Books, an affiliate of Dutton Children's Books, a division of Penguin Books USA Inc., 375 Hudson Street, New York, New York 10014

Editor: Virginia Buckley   Designer: Robin Malkin
Printed in the U.S.A.   First Edition
10 9 8 7 6 5 4 3

FOR
JAMES B. SLAUGHTER
AND
DALE GOLDSMITH

THE POLICE TOOK ME into custody on a cold, wet night in November. I had just finished the grinding climb up Highland Avenue and had turned onto Jefferson for the final mile that would take me back to my house. The night air swished cold through my lungs. Above me leafless oak and maple branches tugged at one another across the street in a battle of long, bony arms. In front of me, Jefferson Road, slick from the drizzle that had been falling off and on for hours, unrolled in a glittering black ribbon. As I picked up my pace, I noticed that a police car was rolling along about half a block behind me.

I started the sprint for home, elbows pumping a steady rhythm. The freezing drizzle began to spatter the roadway, and tiny icy streams ran through my hair over my forehead, eyes, and cheeks. My legs were tired and my breath was stinging, so I stopped thinking about my girlfriend, Kris, and started fantasizing about stomping Igor. This year I would clamp his shoulders to the mat. This season I dreamed I would take his county championship. This year I would be king.

The siren blared out then in a harsh command to halt. The police light cut through the blackness to frame me in midstride. I stopped and waited. The police car stopped ten feet behind me. A policeman got out and walked toward me. He had his right arm extended, and at first, absurdly, I thought he wanted to shake my hand. Then I realized that he was holding a gun.

"What seems to be the problem, Officer?" I asked him, my voice coming in gasps after my long run. My mom had brought me up to treat policemen with a great deal of respect.

He was tall and had a lean face that was half hidden in shadow. As he walked closer, I could see that his eyes were small and quick and were studying me very intently. "Don't move," he said, and stepped yet closer. "Put your arms in the air."

I followed his command, and before I knew it he had frisked me from head to foot in fast, rough movements. I didn't like that at all—not at all, but I kept my mouth shut and stood still. "He's clean, Al," the tall cop called toward the police car. Then the quick eyes turned back to me. "What's your name?"

"Ron Woods."

"What are you doing out tonight?"

"Training. For wrestling season. I always run at night."

"Where did you run?"

"Up Highland to Jefferson."

"Why did you speed up when you saw the police car?"

"I always sprint the last half mile home," I told him.

Then there was a brief silence as he studied me and I examined him. He looked to be about thirty. His hair had begun to thin, but otherwise he looked young and hard. I can tell a lot about someone's condition by the way he looks and by the way he moves, and this tall cop worked out a lot. He stood with his weight evenly balanced on the balls of his feet. I don't know what he saw as he studied me, but he didn't put the gun away, and when he spoke, his voice cracked a sharp order. "Get in the backseat of the car, Ron."

I got into the car. I figured that a mistake was being made and that it would be cleared up real soon. Until then I decided to follow directions. The police car was spotlessly clean. There was a wire grate separating the backseat from the front. I peered through the grate at the driver. He was a short man with a thick neck that widened out to unusually broad shoulders.

The police car began to move. I thought that it was a good time to find out what was going on. "Excuse me, but could you tell me what the problem is?" I asked in as steady a voice as I could manage.

The tall cop turned and looked at me but didn't say a word. He had an unkind face—narrow and steep, like a dangerous ski slope. The driver never took his eyes off the road, but when he spoke, his voice was warm and human.

3

"What's your name, son?"

"Ron Woods."

"Ron, there's been a break-in near here. On Highland Avenue about twenty minutes ago. A serious crime was committed. We're looking for a young man, maybe six foot or six-one, 155 or so, brown hair, wearing sweat pants and a white T-shirt."

I looked down at my black sweat pants and white T-shirt and felt shock waves of icy numbness spreading through my chest. I'm five foot ten and weigh about 150 pounds, and my hair is light brown. "Where are we going?" I asked. I meant to speak in a normal tone, but my voice surprised me by coming out in a loud whisper.

The tall guy still kept silent. The short man turned onto Highland and took a few seconds before answering me. "The intruder left muddy footprints on the kitchen floor of the house. We want to match your shoes against them."

The confidence flowed back in a quick rush. This would all be over soon. They'd take a look at the footprints and realize they had the wrong guy.

The police car stopped in front of a two-story green house. The tall cop got out of the car very quickly and opened the back door for me to climb out. I walked with them toward the house. A few neighbors were standing on the sidewalk, and they stared at me as I walked between the two policemen. I did my best to ignore them. The front yard of the house was a tangle of bushes and vines and tall grass. It smelled musty, and the fringes brushed against my knees as we hurried up the path to the front door.

4

We entered the house. It seemed unnaturally silent. The short cop led me down a long hallway to the kitchen. "Take off your right shoe and lean against that wall," he told me. I handed him the shoe.

The two cops walked with the running shoe toward a far corner of the kitchen, where I could see some muddy brown tracks on the white linoleum floor. The tall cop glanced at me every few seconds. Suddenly and unexpectedly, I got a powerful urge to sprint away. My right leg actually began to move before I caught myself and stood still. The urge passed. The two cops seemed to crouch for a long time by the muddy footprints. Then they turned and came back toward me. The short cop's face was grim and had lost all of its warmth, and when he spoke, each word was snapped like a whip. "The prints match. Ron, you've been here before."

I couldn't speak, so I just shook my head. They looked at me and I looked at them, and the silent accusation and denial might have gone on for a while if an old man hadn't suddenly burst into the room. He must have been seventy, and his shock of white hair was mussed and straggly, as if he had been walking in a strong wind. "Is that him?" he shouted to the policemen. Then, looking right at me, he growled, "What kind of an animal are you to do something like this?"

I looked back at him and had a very odd sensation: I suddenly felt deeply guilty. While on one level I knew I was absolutely innocent of doing this man any harm, on another level I felt just as certain that those staring, accusing eyes must be right, and I must indeed be the culprit. The tall cop hustled the old man out of the room. I was soon in the backseat of the police car

5

as we headed straight for the station. The numbness had spread through my body, and I found myself shivering.

They sat me down at a table and asked me questions.

"Look," I told them, "I'm a straight-A student, and I've never broken a law in my life. I'm captain of the wrestling team and . . ."

"What were you doing on Highland Avenue?" they wanted to know.

"Running. To get in shape for wrestling. I always run hills to build up my legs and wind."

"Did you see anyone?"

"No."

"Talk to anyone?"

"No."

"Hear anything? Anything at all?"

"No," I answered. "Can I call my mother?"

"If we decide to book you. We have our print expert coming in to check out your shoes and the prints. He should be here real soon. Then we'll decide."

The room with the table was bright and bare. The powerful overhead light made me wince and look away. For some reason I had trouble thinking clearly as I sat trying to answer their questions. The light seemed to shine right through my head, and their voices sounded just a tiny bit fuzzy.

Finally, after about thirty minutes, the print expert arrived. I heard them talking to him in the hallway, and then he walked into the room, and I nearly jumped out of my chair with joy and relief. I had known Officer Garrison for at least ten years. He had coached my first Little League team, and he and my mom did a lot of work at the church organizing fund raisers and special community events. He was fifty and just starting to develop a paunch. He looked absolutely baffled to see me sitting there. "Ron, what are you doing here?"

"This is the guy we picked up running away from the house," the tall cop said.

"I was out running for wrestling," I said in a rush. I could feel a few tears burn their way down my cheeks, and I was surprised—I hadn't cried in at least five years.

Garrison came over and put his arm around my shoulders. "I've known this young man for years," he told the other policemen. "He was an eagle scout in the church troop, he's captain of the wrestling team, he's one of the top students in the high school, and he's one of the all-around best young men in this town. You guys better go look for another suspect."

"Take a look at the prints, Garrison," the tall cop suggested.

Garrison looked at him and then at me. Finally he nodded. "Ron, let me just go clear this up," he said. "Then we'll go home, huh?"

I gave him my shoe and waited in the bare, brightly lit room. Officer Garrison was back in less than ten minutes. He smiled at me and shook his head in mock disgust. "They were close, Ron," he said. "A slightly different make of shoe, and one size bigger than yours, but I'd say you've had a very unlucky night. Come on, let's go home."

It felt great to be walking out of the police station

next to a family friend and to climb into the front seat of his car and ride next to him. The numbness that had taken hold of my body in the last few hours melted away.

"You'd be surprised how often this happens," he told me as we drove through the empty streets toward my house. "When you investigate a crime—especially a serious crime—there are always some amazing coincidences. Just try to forget about it, Ron."

I understood what he was trying to say to me, and I decided to let him know that I didn't agree at all. "I didn't like the way they treated me," I told him. "Like I was already guilty. I was innocent, and they really scared me. A couple of coincidences don't give them the right to do that. I had a right to call my mom."

We drove for a while in silence. "Ron," he said, and his tone was rich with sincerity and experience, "I've been a cop for more than twenty years. Every day we try to protect people and uphold the laws. Hell, I've been shot at trying to uphold the law. It's not an easy job." His eyes never strayed from the road as he spoke. He drove carefully and smoothly. "Tonight a serious crime was committed. The police get jumpy when something like that happens. They have to—it goes with their job. Sometimes in order to do right, you have to do a little wrong. Sometimes when there's a lot on the line and you're trying to do the right thing, you have to kind of wink at the law a little bit. Do you understand?"

"No," I told him, and I was surprised at how strong and angry my voice came out, "no, I don't understand. The law is the law. Nobody has a right to wink at it. They should have let me call my mom."

We turned onto Sylvan Avenue, and Officer Garrison slowed the car as we neared my house. It's always a quiet street, and tonight it was absolutely silent and deserted. The only signs of life were the lights that glimmered from the windows of the houses. The air smelled of wet wood.

"Want some advice?" he asked me. I nodded. "Don't tell your mom about this. It'll upset her for nothing. Just go to sleep, and tomorrow morning everything will be back in perspective."

We reached my house. "Thanks for the ride home and for . . . helping me when I needed you," I told him. I opened the door.

Just as I started to get out, he asked a question that I had been half expecting. It's the question everyone asks me. "Ron, are you gonna beat Igor this year?"

"No, he's invincible," I replied, stepping out of the car onto the slick pavement. "But I'm gonna make him suffer a little bit. Bye."

The car drove away, and I was left alone on the quiet street. Our house looked small and old, dwarfed by the much bigger houses on either side of it. I walked up the path and let myself in very quietly—my mom had already gone to sleep. I managed not to wake her as I climbed the stairs and got ready for bed.

My room is very small and filled with all sorts of junk. There are a lot of sports trophies: small old trophies from Little League and from when I used to play ice hockey, bigger trophies from junior high school wrestling tournaments, and then the beautiful silver bowl I got for being the runner up in the county wrestling tournament last year.

My room also has a lot of photographs. There are a couple of me standing next to my mom, taken on various vacations. She photographs very well—she manages to look happy and a bit serious at the same time. I have the same goofy smile in each picture. Then there are two pictures of Kris, one in a skirt and blouse and one in her cheerleading uniform. She's tall and blonde and willowy, and looking at her sometimes makes me think of a glass of lemonade. She's sweet, she's tangy, and there's something refreshing about her open, vulnerable face with its big blue eyes. I don't allow any pictures of my father in my room. My mom once tried to put a picture of him over my desk, but I asked her to take it away.

There are also a couple of hundred books. I read a lot. I like novels, but most of the books that are squeezed onto shelves or stacked up on the floor are either biographies or history books. American history has always drawn me. I can name all the presidents in order and tell you the main events that happened in each of their administrations.

I threaded my way between the stacks of books and climbed into bed, but for a long time I couldn't get to sleep. I kept thinking back to what had happened earlier in the evening and couldn't decide whether it was funny or scary, whether I was amused or angry. Could I blame the police, or was Officer Garrison right and they were just doing their difficult job? Was it sometimes necessary to wink at the law? Why had I felt guilty and even had a strong urge to sprint away? Should I tell my mom about it, or my friends?

I finally decided that I wouldn't tell her but that I would have to tell a few guys on the team. It was too good a story to keep to myself. I knew they'd get a laugh hearing how Ron Woods, the straightest guy in the high school, almost ended up behind bars.

THERE WAS LAUGHTER in The Furnace. It was near the end of our workout, and I had just told some of the guys about my brush with the police. It was odd to hear laughter in hell.

The Furnace is what we call our wrestling room. It's long and narrow and has no windows. The floor is covered with a gray wrestling mat. The ceiling is a tangle of pipes that eventually branches out to bring heat to all the different rooms of the school. When the heat is on and people are working out hard, the temperature in The Furnace can zoom right past a hundred degrees. The pipes often give off loud hissing sounds, and moisture collects on them and drips onto the mats, so it seems like the school building itself is sweating and gasping for air.

Dan "Gorilla" Horton was laughing in loud, belly-shaking bursts. "You?" he demanded, red-faced. "They really took you in for questioning? Mr. Eagle Scout?" His huge, hairy, low-slung gorilla arms dangled down, and shook slightly with every gasp of glee.

"C'mon, I'm not really that straight," I protested. Gorilla is one of my best friends on the team. I've found that most guys who wrestle heavyweight like to laugh and kid around a lot—maybe their size and strength force them to act like clowns so they won't scare people away.

"You're as straight as an arrow, guy," Stinker Williams said, also chuckling. We called him Stinker because he didn't wash his sweat suit very often, and after a week of workouts in The Furnace, Stinker Williams began to win matches on his smell alone.

"You shoulda called me, Ron," Coach Brogan said in his whispery voice. He had been a state championship wrestler in high school and played one year for the Jets; it was a little strange how his mammoth chest and tree-trunk neck produced such a gentle, silvery voice. "I would've bailed you out." He grinned at the thought and then turned back to the team. "Now let's finish up with the last set and some wall-to-wall."

I turned over on my back, and Gorilla clamped my ankles to the mat in a grip of steel. I did my last set of twenty-five sit-ups with a forty-pound weight strapped to my chest. Each time I began a sit-up, I felt my muscles grappling with gravity and gaining inch by inch. I was wearing a warm-up suit on the inside and a rubber sweat suit on the outside, and when I moved I could feel moisture thick and damp across my chest and bands of perspiration around my thighs and legs.

Gorilla rattled out his sit-ups with machine-gun rapidity, his hands clasped behind his head so that his huge biceps looked like they would burst as they pushed his head forward and upward. We finished way ahead of the other pairs of guys. It was our first team workout, and a lot of the guys looked soft. Gorilla and I worked out all year round and were in as good shape today as we would be in midseason. We each had our reasons for pushing ourselves so hard. In this, his senior year, Gorilla had a legitimate shot at the county heavyweight title. And I wanted to make Igor suffer a bit.

Coach Brogan blew his whistle and called the wall-to-wall drill. He went down his clipboard list, matching guys up according to size and power. I drew Carl Stoner. Carl wasn't my favorite guy on the team. He had a sour personality, and on the mat he stretched the rules whenever no one was looking. We had had some real dirty battles in the past. He outweighed me by about ten pounds, and I knew the coach was trying to build up my power by giving me a heavier opponent.

Four pairs of wrestlers did the wall-to-wall drill at the same time. We started at one wall of the long, narrow room, facing the far wall across the mat. I started off in the down position on all fours, with Carl kneeling over me with his right arm across my chest and his left hand on my left elbow. I could feel that he had gotten stronger during the off-season. His right arm, though relaxed, circled my chest with a promise of great power.

Coach Brogan explained the drill for the new kids. "The wall-to-wall is simple," he told them. "When I

14

blow the whistle, the guy in the down position will have thirty seconds to try to make it across the room to the far wall. He can crawl, roll, try to stand, or whatever else works. The guy on top has to try to break him down and keep him from getting across. Any questions?" There were none. Coach Brogan put the whistle in his mouth, held his stopwatch up in his right hand, and blew.

Carl tried to break me down. His left arm yanked up my left arm while his right arm, with the weight of his body behind it, tried to grind me into the mat. He didn't quite have the strength. I like to let my opponent commit himself, so I gave Carl two or three seconds. His weight was pressing down on the center of my back as he tried to yank up my arm and hook my legs to bring me down. I pretended to give way a bit, and then when I felt him shift his weight, I ducked my right side down and powered everything into a surge with my left leg. Sure enough, he lost his balance and almost flipped off. He managed to stay on top by bracing his legs out to either side, but I started peeling off his hands and spinning my body away from him. He desperately clutched for a grip, and the fingernails of his right hand raked across my forehead. I successfully threw him off and was the first to make it to the other side of the room. My teammates who had been watching applauded. I touched my hand to my forehead, and it came away red with blood from three or four gashes.

Carl had chased me across the mat, and now he was standing near me, looking embarrassed at how quickly I had gone wall-to-wall. "Why don't you cut your nails?" I demanded.

"You moved before the whistle," he shot back. "You made me look bad."

Fifteen seconds had passed. None of the other wrestlers had made it across. Suddenly, with five seconds left to go, Gorilla managed to stand up and stagger across the room. He carried the poor guy who was trying to restrain him on his broad shoulders. We clapped as Gorilla touched the wall with only one second left and lowered his red-faced opponent to the mat.

We switched it around immediately, so that no one had any time to rest. This time I was in the up position. I could feel Carl tensing his back and legs beneath me, getting ready to surge at the sound of the whistle. The blood from my forehead ran into my eyes, causing a salty burn. I blinked several times and concentrated. He wasn't going anywhere.

At the sound of the whistle, I used his forward jolt to ride him into the mat. I quickly controlled his legs and wrenched his arm out, and soon he was all tied up. The seconds ticked off. He flailed, but it was hopeless. Then his thumb dug into my windpipe like a dagger. I let go and fell off as I gasped and tried to breathe. He got up and ran across the room. It took me a few seconds to get my breath and clear my head, but then I got up and headed for him. He saw me coming and backed up a step. "It was an accident, Ron," he said. "I didn't mean to thumb ya."

My eyes were still tearing from the pain. I had definitely lost control. I pushed him back into the wall of the wrestling room. He fell against the wall hard and came up swinging. I ducked a looping right and took a weak left to the forehead as I stepped inside

16

and let go with a quick combination. Right, left, right, and even though he was sinking down, I would have thrown more punches if Coach Brogan hadn't caught my arm and hauled me off.

Carl got up slowly. "What's he hittin' me for? Same team," Carl said.

"I saw your thumb," Coach Brogan told him. "We don't need that stuff here." Then he looked at me. "Don't you ever lose control like that again. You tell me if you're fouled, and I'll take care of it. Understood? Both of you?"

We both nodded. We were looking into each other's eyes, and the anger flowed back and forth.

Practice ended a few minutes later. "Everyone, listen up," Coach Brogan said before he dismissed us. "The day after tomorrow all of you have to come to the nurse's office at ten o'clock."

"But we already had our physicals," somebody pointed out.

"The nurse wants to give Gorilla another hernia test," Stinker Williams joked.

"Hey, Nurse Peterson and I are just good friends," Gorilla responded. "Although I must say I like mature women." That got a laugh, because Nurse Peterson was pushing seventy.

"This is important," Coach Brogan said, and his gentle whisper sliced through our chatter and quieted the team. "The county athletic association has a new policy on drug testing. All varsity athletes are going to be tested for drugs. I want to make it clear that this is for your own good. If any of you have been doing anything with drugs that could make your participation

17

on this team dangerous to your health, I want to know about it."

There was a silence. This was totally new.

"This test . . . doesn't test for alcohol?" Van Roberts asked. Van was a heavy partier during the off-season.

"No, it doesn't," Coach Brogan answered. "Alcohol dissolves too quickly into the blood for it to be tested. Unless you drank a beer for breakfast that day, alcohol would never show up."

"I'll stick to orange juice," Van promised.

"What'll you do if you catch somebody?" Stinker Williams asked, and the room suddenly got very quiet.

"It's not so much catching someone as trying to protect and help him," Coach Brogan told us. "There was a football player last year at Cougar High, Tom Powers, you might have read about him. Dropped dead in the middle of a game. It turned out he was using a couple of drugs that put an unnatural strain on his heart. If there's anyone in our program like that, I don't want to punish him or embarrass him—I want to help him. As far as I'm concerned, if anyone tests positive, I'd like to keep it very private, arrange for some rehabilitative counseling, and get him back on the team as soon as possible."

There were no more questions. The team headed for the locker room. I felt kind of bad about getting into a fight with a teammate, so I showered and dressed fast. Gorilla and Stinker Williams joined me on the walk home.

"You had every right in the world to clock him,"

Gorilla told me. "Coach saw the thumb, so don't worry about it."

"Yeah, but I'm the captain this year. I shouldn't fight. . . ."

"Stoner's a crumb," Stinker Williams cut me off. "Somebody had to teach him. Don't give it a second thought."

"All right," I agreed. "Let's talk about something else."

"I've heard about this drug testing stuff before, but I never thought they'd try it at our school," Gorilla mused.

"Seems like a good idea to me," Stinker said. "Doubt they'll find anyone on our team."

"I don't like it at all," I told them quickly. "I've heard about it, too, and I've read some articles for it and against it. I don't think a high school has a right to test you this way."

"But it could save someone's life," Stinker argued.

"Even so," I said. "You guys know I read a lot about American history and the Constitution. Some things in this country are sacred. You can't force people to take tests like that, even if it's for their own good."

We reached Stinker's house. He lives in a small one-story ranch-style home with picture windows facing out on the street. He's got a big front yard, which we used to play tackle football in when we were kids. I don't think the grass has ever completely grown back from those games.

"What're you guys up to tonight?" Stinker asked. "Wanna get together?"

Gorilla nodded, and they both looked at me when I shook my head. "Got a date with Kris," I told them. Kris and I had only been going out for three weeks, and Stinker and Gorilla were just getting used to the fact that I now spent a lot of my free time with her.

"Hey, all right," Stinker said with a whistle. "Senior woman, probably knows a lot of tricks. You like those older women, huh, guy?"

"Hey, he's a fighter and a lover," Gorilla said.

"Let's hope I can keep them separate," I told him.

"Where you gonna take her?" Stinker wanted to know.

"Just out for a drive. She just got her license, so we're gonna celebrate."

"Hey, senior cheerleader chauffeur service. Sounds great," Stinker said. "Just don't let her take you down to the reservoir."

"I can swim," I told him, blushing and grinning at the same time.

"If she gets you down there, she's gonna drown you in love. Take care of yourself, stud. I think you got big things coming tonight. That drug test won't pick up recent sex, will it?"

"No," I told him, "but if you don't wash your sweats soon, you may be the first person in history to fail on smell alone."

"Bye, lover boy," he said and went into his house.

"WHY DON'T WE DRIVE down to the reservoir?"
Kris asked me. She turned her head, and for a moment
I looked right into those sparkling blue eyes that
seemed alive the way firelight seems alive. Deep down
in my stomach I felt a twinge of unease that quickly
twisted into a cold knot of fear. I nodded, and she
smiled and turned the car downhill.

Up till then it had been a perfect evening. Kris had
come over to my house to eat dinner and meet my
mother. Mom had fixed one of her fancy French din-
ners and served it on her fine wedding china. She really did it up, so that we dined by candlelight with
classical music playing softly in the background, and
our dining room seemed transformed into a fancy restaurant.

My mom is still a very beautiful and young-looking

woman. She married my dad when she graduated from high school, and now, twenty years later, there isn't a wrinkle on her face or a gray hair in her head. Despite her youthful looks, my mom is very old-fashioned, which is why, I guess, I've turned out to be so straight and conservative. It was Mom's idea to invite Kristene over for dinner. "I can't believe you're really Ron's mother—you look more like his older sister," Kris told her during the meal.

My mother smiled at her and then replied with her usual forthright honesty. "I'm thirty-eight years old, but thank you for the compliment. Ron didn't tell me you were a flatterer."

"Just honest," Kris replied.

"Good," Mom said simply. "Honesty is the quality I value most highly in people. Especially in friends of my son." When she spoke the word *friends,* my mom smiled, and an odd tone in her voice reflected a strong emotion.

I saw that they really liked each other, so I relaxed and just enjoyed the meal. The onion soup was thick with onions and had a layer of tasty cheese melted across the top in a kind of crust. The main dish, duckling *à l'orange,* arrived on a bed of hot rice garnished with pineapple, apricots, and watercress. I usually eat small portions because I have to keep my weight down for wrestling, but tonight I couldn't resist a second serving of wonderfully glazed duckling. For dessert we went into the living room and had strong coffee and some French pastries my mother had baked. I limited myself to half a pastry.

22

The only awkward minute in the whole dinner came when Kris pointed up at the picture of my father that hangs to one side of the fireplace. "Is that Ron's father?" she asked my mom. "He's so handsome in uniform."

I turned away and couldn't suppress a little scowl. Why did Kris have to bring up my dad at the end of a perfectly happy dinner?

"Yes, he was a very handsome man. Like his son," my mother said gently.

I knew her eyes were on me, but I kept watching the cracks in the floor. "I don't look like him at all," I muttered. "Not at all."

There was a silence. Then Kris spoke to my mother in an attempt to break through the momentary awkwardness. She didn't ask it outright, but she touched on the only question in the whole world that can make my mother squirm. "You're so young-looking and so nice and such a great cook. . . ." Kris said, and her eyes swung from the photograph of my dad to my mom's face.

"You're wondering why I never remarried?" my mother asked the question for her. She drew in a deep breath. "I've thought of it. But I could never get up the strength to take that picture down from its spot next to the hearth. For me, it always seemed to belong there, like a cornerstone of this house."

Kris nodded and sipped her coffee in silence. My mom went back to the kitchen to get another pastry. I reached over and sifted the blonde hair that glitters as it flows down Kris's back in a golden stream. She smiled at me, put her hand over my hand, and then we both moved away a bit as my mother came back into the room.

"Take a look at my car," Kris invited my mother after dinner. It was a cute red Honda Civic CR2, and I could tell that Kris was very proud of it.

"It's beautiful," my mom told her. "Congratulations on getting your license."

"Yeah, let's just hope she knows how to drive," I said, getting into the passenger seat.

"Good-bye, Mrs. Woods. Thank you for a delicious dinner," Kris said. The little engine roared into life, and we were off, whizzing down Sylvan Avenue.

We drove around town for a while, and, like Stinker Williams had said, I kind of enjoyed being chauffeured around by a beautiful senior cheerleader. A crowd of kids in front of the Pizza Spot craned their necks to figure out who we were as we drove by, honking loudly. Kris U-turned and came back the other way, and this time they figured it out and applauded her new car.

Now we were on narrow Reservoir Road, slicing our way between the night shadows of giant pines. Kris drove in silence, occasionally throwing quick glances at me. I guess she could tell that I was tense. The reservoir is the most famous make-out spot in town. I'd never taken this trip before. A breeze tapped branches against the car windows. I'd never made out with a girl in my life. An owl hooted nearby, a weird, primeval sound. To tell the truth, Kristene was the first girl I'd ever gone out with.

Ahead, the reservoir glinted black in the moonlight

like a puddle of oil. We were getting close. The trees thinned out on either side. Was it my imagination, or was there suddenly a faint new smell in the car, a sweetness like perfume but at the same time different from perfume? Kris was breathing a little bit harder, and I was surprised to feel one of my feet suddenly cramp up. I pressed it down on the floor of the car, and the cramp gradually went away.

Kris seemed to know just where she was going. Now we were off Reservoir Road, rolling slowly along a thin path that skirted one of the reservoir's banks. I realized that Kris had been to this spot before. For the last two years she had gone out with Tommy Faye, our school's star running back. This year Tommy had gone off to Wake Forest on a football scholarship, and Kris had found herself in her senior year without a boyfriend. As we rolled along, I wondered whom Tommy had found out about this spot from. And how had Kris felt the first time she had come down here?

Kris stopped the car in a grove of pine trees. I rolled down my window. The November air was sharply cold and sweet with the green smell of pine needles. We sat there in silence for a few seconds. Kris turned on the car radio real low. "I really like your mom," she finally said.

"Yeah, she's neat," I agreed. My voice sounded like it was coming up in rattles and gasps through a twenty-foot-long metal pipe.

"And I like you," Kris said. "I really do."

"Yeah, I like you too," I managed to get out.

"I mean, you seem so much more serious than the other guys your age. You seem deeper."

25

Her hand touched my knee, sending shock waves up my thigh. My brain was barely functioning. "I've never been down here before at night. It's . . . so quiet," I mumbled.

This time her hand stayed on my knee. Her other hand tiptoed through the hairs on the back of my neck. "Do you know what drives me crazy when I look at you?" she asked.

"My smile? Everyone says I have a goofy smile," I babbled. The old brain was definitely going at one mile per hour.

"I like your body," she said with a little laugh. "So tough. Every muscle locked into place. Let me feel it." Her hand ran lightly down my body from neck to waist.

"It's like that 'cause I work out a lot," I heard my own voice say. On some deep level of consciousness I found myself marveling at the stupidity of what I was saying.

"Ron," she asked, "would you like to kiss me?"

"Would I like to?" I repeated. "Would I like to kiss you?" We had exchanged a few quick kisses over the past three weeks, but I knew she was talking about something very different.

"Yes, would you like to kiss me? You can if you want." She moved close to me. Her long blonde hair brushed against my face in a magically light veil.

Slowly I reached out and put my arm around her, and she sort of scooted into my lap. Our lips touched. Her breath was sweet and her lips were soft and the kiss must have lasted for five steamy minutes. I broke for a breath of air.

"I really like you," she whispered as she took my hand and pressed it against her breast. I stroked gently, feeling the soft silk of her shirt rubbing against the stiffness of her bra, which shielded the soft, pliant mound underneath. I reached up and undid the buttons of her shirt one by one. It took a long time because my fingers were shaking. I put my hand inside her shirt and up underneath her bra. She was really breathing now. Her nipple was hard.

"Ouch, you're hurting me," she gasped and pulled away for a second. She gave me a strange smile. "Here, this should help." She undid the clasps of her bra and slipped it off. Her firm breasts seemed to be reaching out toward me. "Now be gentle," she whispered, coming close. "You animal."

Soon she was back on my lap. We kissed, and this time her tongue crept into my mouth. I met it with my own tongue, and the probing and flickering sensation was delicious. She took my hand and pulled it down to her legs. She guided it under the hem of her skirt and along her thigh till my fingers brushed her panties. She gave a little moan and began fumbling at my belt.

And that was when I kind of rocked her off and opened the car door and bolted away to a tree by the water's edge. I stood leaning against the tree, trying to get my breath.

Kris stayed in the car. After a few minutes she called out in a soft voice, "Ron? Are you okay?"

"Yeah," I called back.

"Why don't you come back to the car?"

"No," I said.

"Can I come over there and talk to you?"

"Kris . . ." I began but didn't know how to finish. I still wasn't thinking very clearly.

She got out of the car and walked over to me. She had put her shirt back on. "Can I ask you a question?" She waited for a second and then asked in a very soft voice, "Is this the first time you ever made out?"

I nodded.

"You were doing great," she said. "You had me all worked up."

"I guess we both kind of lost control," I said.

"Well, why'd you stop?" she asked, and her voice was somewhere between curiosity and playfulness.

It took me a few seconds to think of an answer. "Because I like to be the one making the decisions. Doing the leading."

"Okay," she said. "Let's go back into the car, and this time you make the decisions."

"Well . . . no," I told her. "No. Not tonight."

"Why not?"

"Because I don't think we know each other well enough."

Then a giggle kind of popped out of her mouth before she could stifle it. "Ron, why don't you admit it?"

"What?"

"That you haven't done this before, and you're a little afraid."

"I'm not afraid."

"You ran out of that car like you were terrified," she said, and I could tell another giggle was on its way.

I got angry. "Well, some girls might not want to

seem so knowledgeable about sex. As if they've done everything billions of times before."

There was a long silence. "Get in the car," she finally said, and her voice sounded very different. "I want to leave."

"You sound mad now."

I was surprised when she shouted, *"I am mad."* She took a second to quiet down. "I'm eighteen years old, and I've had only one boyfriend, who I went out with for more than two years and really loved. And you make me sound like a . . . slut."

She walked back to the car. I followed her and got in the passenger side. She switched on the ignition, and the car rolled out of the grove of trees toward Reservoir Road.

For a few minutes we drove in silence. "Kristene," I said.

"What?"

"I'm sorry we had a fight. I didn't mean that you were a slut."

She didn't say anything. We turned off Reservoir Road onto Main Street. Neon signs from stores shimmered in the distance. "I think you're terrific," I told her. "And I really enjoyed dinner tonight. I could tell that my mom liked you."

"I enjoyed dinner too," she admitted.

"Let's go out again soon," I told her. "Let's just do something fun so we can forget all about this . . . bad night."

"Okay," she said. "Here's your house."

"You're not still angry?"

29

"No," she said. "I still like you, Ron. You have a special quality. Maybe that's what I like so much about you. Your reputation is absolutely true."

I had the car door open. "What's my reputation?" I asked her.

"That you're the straightest guy in the school. That you never drink or smoke or break any rules at all."

"Could the straightest guy in the school kiss you good night?" I asked her.

She leaned over, and my quick good-night kiss turned into a prolonged smooch. "Good night, Ron," she finally said.

I got out of the car and closed the door gently. "Good night, Kris."

"COACH BROGAN, could I talk to you for a minute?" He was on the phone, so I stayed outside the phys ed office, waiting for him to finish talking. He hung up the phone and gestured for me to come in.

"What's up?"

I sat down in a chair near the trophy case. The case is huge and contains all the trophies our school's teams have won in the past ten years. Many of them are wrestling trophies. Coach Brogan knows how to put winning teams together.

He was sitting as he always does, his back ramrod straight and his massive arms loose at his sides. If they gave awards for good posture, Coach Brogan would walk away with all of them. There's something about the stiff discipline with which he carries himself that I can identify with—Coach Brogan is the only guy in school whose hair is as short as mine.

"I want to ask you a hypothetical question," I told him. "Something's been kind of bothering me."

"What's your question?"

"Well, you know that new drug test that we're all supposed to take tomorrow?" He nodded. "What would happen—hypothetically—if I decided not to take it?"

His deep-set gray eyes studied me carefully. "I wouldn't be able to let you wrestle on the team this year."

"Even though you know I don't use drugs or drink or anything like that? Even though you trust me?"

"Ron, the point is, it's not my decision. It's a new countywide rule. No drug test, no participation." He picked up a small rubber ball and squeezed it in his palm as he talked to me. With each squeeze, the biceps corded together on his arm. "Why do you ask?"

"Well," I told him, "you know, it really bothered me the other night when the police took me in as a suspect and treated me like I was already guilty. I did a paper on the McCarthy hearings last semester, and I couldn't believe how easily people's constitutional rights were violated. Since then I've been reading about other cases where the government has ignored people's rights. Like tapping people's phones or searching their homes without a proper warrant. I don't like the idea of some county athletic board telling me I've got to give a sample of my urine for analysis. It's like they're searching the inside of my body. I don't think they have the right to do that."

32

Coach Brogan looked thoughtful for a minute. He put the small rubber ball aside and rubbed his chin with his large right hand. "To some extent I agree with you," he said. "I don't like being told what to do either. On the other hand, as a coach, the information from these tests might help me save the life of one of my wrestlers. That death last year at Cougar High during a football game . . . that was a real tragedy."

"Something might seem beneficial, but if it goes against our rights as citizens, then we should oppose it," I told him.

He stood up and walked closer to me. He sat on a desk a few feet away. "Ron, you're scaring me. We have a good shot at the county team title this year. If you don't take that test, you can't wrestle. It's that simple."

"You really think we can win the county?"

"Yes," he said, "I do."

"Do you think I can beat Igor?"

Coach Brogan is always absolutely honest when he talks about wrestling. He shook his head. "Not this year. He's too strong. If he were a junior now, so you had a season and a summer to build up, you might be able to take him next year. This year I think you're gonna give him a good fight, but I think he's invincible."

"But you think I can give him a good fight?"

"I think you're gonna give him a damn good fight."

The phone in the office rang. "Don't worry, I'm gonna take the test," I told Coach Brogan as he got up to answer it. "Otherwise, I'd never know about Igor."

"There's another factor, too," Coach Brogan told me. "If you decided not to take the test, I'd be so

33

angry I'd probably try to rip you in half." Coming from a man with nineteen-inch biceps, that was a persuasive argument.

I must have really scared Coach Brogan, because sometime during the course of the day he mentioned our conversation to a couple of my friends on the team. Stinker Williams began to apply pressure as we waited our turn for rope drill. "I heard a rumor about you today," he told me.

At first I thought he had heard something about what had happened between Kris and me the previous night. I felt myself blush and turned my face away for a second. "What did ya hear?"

"I heard that you're toying with the idea of not taking the drug test."

My whole body relaxed. "I'm probably gonna take it," I told him. "I just don't like being forced to do it."

"Yeah? Well, you might be looking at this whole thing too seriously. I mean, Ron, tomorrow we'll go down and piss into a test tube, and hand it over to a doctor, and that's it. Over. Finished. Then we can start concentrating on a terrific season."

Coach Brogan blew his whistle. Eight ropes hung down from a metal support that glittered high up near the gymnasium's ceiling. I grabbed a rope and waited for the second whistle. Stinker was on one side of me, and a heavyweight named Ladd was on the other side. I feel sorry for the heavyweights when it comes to rope drill. The lighter you are, the easier it is to challenge gravity.

The second whistle sounded, sharp and shrill. I

began to climb, one hand hanging on while I reached for a grip higher up the rope. My arms felt very strong, and I was at the top of the rope in a few seconds. I touched the metal support and then came down quickly, slowing myself just enough to avoid rope burn. As soon as my feet touched the floor, I began my second climb. The poor heavyweight on my left was still finishing his slow first ascent. Stinker Williams, on my right, was almost even with me, but I knew I'd smoke him on the third climb. My arms were beginning to feel it a little by the time I reached the top, but I dropped back down in a smooth, controlled glide.

The third climb was the hardest one because we weren't allowed to use our legs. I kept my legs kicked out straight to either side as I hauled myself up with arm strength alone. A lot of the guys couldn't finish the third climb, but my challenge was to make it without slowing or varying my pace in any way. I touched the top and came down just a little too fast, so my right hand suddenly tingled from a small rope burn.

The other seven guys were still climbing. I liked being first. I had worked for years to get into this kind of shape, and I enjoyed finishing rope drill and not even feeling tired.

"Hey, I'm supposed to be the monkey on this team," Gorilla said. "You climb too fast."

"No, you're not a monkey," I told him. "Monkeys are small. You're a member of the large African ape species."

"You should be narrating 'Wild Kingdom,'" he told me. "Any other useful information?"

"Well, you might enjoy knowing that the word *gorilla* comes from the Greek word *gorillai,* which refers to a tribe of hairy women." I file away these bits of trivia about gorillas to taunt the big guy.

Gorilla grinned. "Really? A tribe of hairy women? Sounds kinky, but I wouldn't mind being captured and subjected to weird tribal rituals."

"You have a one-track mind," I told him. It's true. When Gorilla starts talking about sex, you cannot get him off the subject.

"Which brings us to the question of what happened on the banks of the reservoir last night," Gorilla said with an expectant leer.

"Yeah, I was surprised you could climb the ropes so well after such a long night of love," Stinker said, joining the conversation.

"How do you guys know we even went to the reservoir?" I asked them.

"Spike Corliss saw Kris's car turn off on Reservoir Road about ten o'clock," Gorilla told me. "I assume she wasn't going down there alone to do some night fishing."

Stinker smirked. "C'mon, details, details."

"Sorry, guys," I told them. "Last night was a personal thing. I'm gonna keep it to myself."

"He doesn't think he can trust us," Stinker Williams said to Gorilla.

Gorilla nodded. "I'm hurt," he said. "I'm deeply offended."

"Hey, if one of you guys ever gets a girlfriend, maybe you'll understand the need for privacy," I told them and walked away.

Coach Brogan was marking on his clipboard the names of the wrestlers who hadn't been able to finish the third climb. "You can sleep easy," I told him. "I'm gonna take the test."

"Good," he said. "And I hope you can get some sleep too."

"What do you mean?"

He grinned at me. "I hear you're the new king of the reservoir. Just don't tire yourself out, Love God."

I WAS THE FIFTH ONE to be tested. It took about twenty seconds. Nurse Peterson called my name, and a man from the drug testing service handed me a test tube and led me to a toilet stall that had had its door removed. "Why do you need to watch?" I asked him.

"These tests can be beat pretty easily if the urine donor has a chance to introduce an outside substance into his sample. So we have to monitor the testing."

I filled up the test tube and handed it to him. He checked that my name was Ron Woods and attached a sticker that was coded by number to the test tube. While the process was quick and simple and painless, I couldn't get over a nagging feeling that I was doing something wrong—something I didn't condone. It felt disgusting and degrading to have to urinate into a test tube with a man watching to make sure I didn't slip something into my sample. I had promised people that I would take the test, and I had come this far, so I figured I might as well hand in the sample. But I decided then and there that I would never take such a test again. In the future the county would have to find another way of fighting the drug problem in school athletics.

My wrestling teammates were all gathered outside the nurse's office, joking and waiting their turns. "How was it, Love God?" Gorilla wanted to know. "Was it good for you?"

"I think you got the concept wrong," I told him. "You're supposed to urinate into it, not beat off."

"Hey, I better drink some more water," Stinker Williams said. "I'm afraid I may not be able to fulfill my manly duty."

Just then the fire bell rang. The metal clanging seemed to echo back and forth through the basement hallway, louder and louder. We headed up a flight of stairs and out a side exit. Long lines of students were already beginning to fill the sidewalks around the school.

By chance I ended up near Kris. She gave me a big smile. She was wearing jeans and a V-neck red sweater, and the sight of her made me catch my breath. "Hi," she said, "glad to see you escaped from the fire."

"Think it's real?"

"Definitely. A burner fell over in chem lab. A couple of papers caught, and the smoke set off the alarm."

"You look great in that sweater," I told her.

"Thank you."

"Are you ready for another strange evening with

39

the straightest guy in New Jersey?" I asked in a low voice so no one else would hear.

"I wouldn't want to spend tonight with anyone else," she replied with a grin.

"There's a classic movie at the drive-in."

"What's it called?"

"Oh, it's got a name like *Monsters from Mars Meet Vampire Punk Rockers,*" I told her.

"I see," she said. "Sounds like a real classic."

"You don't want to go?"

"Of course I want to go," she said with a warm smile. "I want to see what your idea of a fun evening is."

"Leave it to me," I told her. "After the movie maybe we can go for some late night bowling."

She grimaced. "Well, I'm glad you told me. Now I'll know not to wear a dress. I guess I'm just lucky I fell for such a classy guy."

"I THOUGHT YOU were kidding," Kris said as we turned into the Bowler City parking lot.

"I never kid," I told her. "You know I'm a serious kind of guy."

"Who goes bowling at eleven o'clock at night?"

"All the best people," I assured her. "I just hope we can get a lane."

"Well, if we can't, we can just go someplace else," she said as she guided her little car into a parking place.

"Kris, you'll love it," I promised. "It's not like normal bowling. It's an . . . event."

Midnight Bowling Madness is a new concept at Bowler City, and it seems to be catching on. From eleven o'clock to one in the morning the overhead lights are turned off, so that the only lights in the huge

41

building come from above the lanes and over the pins. Loud rock music is pumped in through huge speakers, and for five dollars you can bowl as many games as you want.

"Okay, it's different," Kris admitted as she laced up her bowling shoes. "I like the music." Springsteen's "Born in the USA" was thumping through the bowling alley. Bowler City was already half full, and more people kept coming in by the minute.

"You haven't bowled much before?" I asked her.

"Just a few times. I'm not a bowling pro or anything."

"Well, let me give you a few pointers. First, always try to start your approach from the same place. When you release the ball, you should be looking at the pocket where you want the ball to end up. Always finish with a smooth follow-through. Here, like this." I got set, took a quick three-step approach, and bowled my strong left-handed hook. It broke late, and two pins remained standing.

"Very impressive," she admitted. I knocked down the two pins with my second ball and then gestured for her to roll a practice frame.

She started kind of far forward. "You might want to start back another step to give yourself a full three-step approach," I suggested.

She smiled at me. "Thanks, but I'm comfortable from here." Then she turned back to face the pins, went into an absolutely smooth approach, and rolled a perfectly controlled hook that smashed the pocket for a perfect strike.

"I guess maybe you didn't need the lessons," I said.

42

"I guess maybe I didn't," she agreed. "What did you say you wanted to bet on this game?"

We bet an ice cream soda on two out of three games and split the first two, so it came down to the third one. I finally managed to beat her and win the bet, but only by five pins. Every game she threw was above 140, and she was usually pushing 150. I liked the way she hadn't let on that she knew anything about bowling and then turned out to be so good. I enjoy being with people who can keep me guessing.

"My dad used to take us bowling when we were little," she told me as we sipped ice cream sodas. Kris's parents were divorced, and this was the first time she had talked to me about her father. "Dad owned a part interest in a bowling alley on Route 7, so we got to bowl for free. If you think I'm good now, you should have seen me then. I was a tiny terror."

"What does your dad do now?" I asked her.

"He's in Europe," she said. "I get a letter from him every once in a while. He's opened a restaurant over there, and he's making a lot of money. He sent me the money for my new car as a combined eighteenth-birthday present and graduation present."

"Is it weird?" I asked her. "Thinking about your mother and father separately because they live such different lives?"

"It was when I was little, but I'm used to it now. It's not like my dad and mom are enemies or anything. They talk. They just weren't happy together."

It was a huge ice cream soda. I was only about half finished, and I'd been drinking steadily while she talked.

"Can I ask about your dad?" she said in a timid voice. "I'd like to know. . . ."

"What's there to talk about?" I asked her, and my voice was suddenly sharp. "He was a jerk."

"Why do you say that?"

"Because he was. Threw away his life in the dumbest war in the history of the world. What a fool."

Kris was looking at me strangely. "Did you ever know him?"

"No, I never knew him," I said, and my voice came out much too loud. The people at the next table looked over. "He died when I was eight months old. He never even saw me."

"Well, your mother doesn't think he was foolish," Kris said. "I could see how much she still loves him—after all these years. When she looks at his picture, she gets a light in her eyes. . . ."

I got up from the table and hurried into the men's room. I sloshed some cold water on my face and took a few deep breaths. By the time I walked back to the table, Kris had finished her soda and was ready to leave. She was smart enough not to say anything.

We got in her car and rolled away from Bowler City.

We both kept silent. It was late, and the streets were dark and deserted. "I'm sorry if I said something I shouldn't have," Kris said in a very low voice.

"It's me, not you," I answered.

She took her right hand off the steering wheel to trace her fingers lightly down my left shoulder and arm. "Where do you want to go now?" she asked.

44

"I'd better go home," I told her. "Gotta get to bed or I'll fall asleep in wrestling practice tomorrow."

"Okay," she said. She sounded just a little bit disappointed. She popped a tape in the stereo, and some slow, beautiful jazz pulsed though the car, with sad saxophones and tortured trombones.

We soon reached my house. "I had a good time tonight," she said. "The movie was fun, and I haven't bowled in years."

I gave her a quick good-night kiss and started to get out. Then I climbed back in. "Kris, I'm sorry we're not more alike. I try, but . . . it seems like you want a boyfriend who's a lot wilder and crazier than I am."

"If a guy and girl are too much alike, things get dull," she told me. "You're interesting. And I really did have fun. Honestly. I just wish I had beaten you at bowling."

"We all have our dreams," I told her with a little grin. Spontaneously I reached for her and she leaned toward me, and I gave her a good-night kiss that lasted for quite a while. The slow jazz vibrated through the small car, and I felt that during the kiss we somehow got to know and like and understand each other a lot better.

She finally broke away. "I don't want your mom seeing the car out here and wondering what's going on. You'd better go."

"You know," I told her, "tonight was the first time I ever talked about my father. It was painful, but I'm glad we can talk about things like that."

"Me too," Kris said. "Good night, Ron."

Coach Brogan called me into his office during sixth period. It was the first time since I had known him that he had looked upset and quite nervous. He was pacing the cluttered room, swerving around piles of sports equipment and desks and chairs. "Come on in," he said when he saw me. "And close the door."

I wasn't sure I had heard him right. The door to the phys ed office was always propped wide open. "What?"

"Close the door, Ron," he repeated. "I think we should talk in private."

I closed the door and sat down in an ugly orange armchair. "What's up?" I asked.

He looked at me and then away at the case of sports trophies. His fingers were all wrapped up in a knot, and when his knuckles cracked, it sounded like small bones were snapping. Suddenly he came over and stood directly above me. "I want you to know that I trust you one hundred percent," he told me. "I don't have a son, but if I did, I think I would feel the same way about him that I feel about you."

I didn't know what was coming, but I knew it was going to be something serious. I waited.

"Ron, have you ever used drugs? Have you even smoked one joint in the last few weeks? Even a few small puffs?"

"I've never used any drugs at all in my whole life," I told him, looking him straight in the eye.

He let out a breath. "I know that," he said. "Listen, the testing agency found traces of marijuana in your urine."

For a second I froze, but the fear quickly melted and gave way to a feeling of great calmness and certainty. I knew I had never used drugs. "There was something wrong with the test," I told him.

"I agree," he said quickly. "I contacted the testing agency, and they said you should come in for a retest. They claim their test is extremely accurate, but they said that whenever someone tests positive they recommend an immediate retest." He paused for a second. His voice became stronger and more confident. "I set it up for tomorrow morning at ten. I'll get you out of class and drive you over to the testing center myself."

"You arranged all that?" I asked him.

"Sure," he said. "And you should know something

47

else. Rumors have a way of spreading, and harmful secrets have a way of leaking, so I made very sure that absolutely no one else in this school found out the results of your first test. That includes the principal and the athletic director. So we'll drive in tomorrow and take the retest and clear this whole thing up. It will be like it never happened. Okay?"

I knew instantly what I was going to have to do, but I was afraid to tell the coach, so I just sat there.

"Okay?" he asked again.

I stood up to face him. "I don't believe in mandatory drug testing," I told him. "I've never used a drug in my life, and I think you know that, so it's not because I'm afraid or anything. I didn't want to take the first test, but I got talked and pressured into it. While I was taking it, I felt like I was betraying my own morals. I don't think I want to take the test again."

The skin around the corners of his mouth quivered just a little. "Ron," he said, and somehow the tone of his voice turned my name into an argument and an appeal. "Ron."

I shook my head.

Just then the basketball coach knocked and pushed the door open. "Okay if I come in?" he asked. "Gotta get some stuff."

"Sure," Coach Brogan told him. "Ron, are you gonna be home tonight?" he asked me. I nodded. "Can I come over and talk to you after dinner? Maybe eight o'clock?"

"Sure," I told him. "Maybe we can think of something."

"I'm sure we can," he said. "Like I said, I think this is our year to take a shot at the county title. We can't let problems get in our way."

"See you at eight," I told him and walked out of the office.

The rest of the day slid by in agonizingly slow segments. I went to all my classes, but instead of thinking about schoolwork, my mind kept returning to the question of the test. Why had I tested positive? Could the lab have slipped up somehow? I tried to convince myself again and again that there was nothing wrong with agreeing to the retest. What did my own opinion on an ethical question matter? The important thing was the team. The important thing was not to make waves. I owed a winning season to Coach Brogan and to my teammates who had worked so hard to reach this level of strength and skill. And even as I tried to convince myself with these arguments, I knew in the back of my mind that if I took the retest I would lose a lot of my self-respect. I knew how I felt deep down—to take the test would mean selling out.

Wrestling practice went by slowly. No one on the team knew, and as I sweated through the various phases of our workout, I became more and more conscious of how much I was at the very center of this team. As captain, I led the stretching exercises. I set the standard in rope climbing. Gorilla and I were the two wrestlers everyone watched during the wall-to-wall drill. Two freshman wrestlers even came up to me with questions about technique during our ten-minute rest break.

49

I told my mother during dinner. When she heard that my sample had tested positive for marijuana, she shook her head and said, "That's patently ridiculous."

I explained to her how they wanted me to take a retest and how I planned to refuse. "You believe me. The coach believes me. Everyone at school knows me and knows that I don't do drugs at all. That trust is the real test as far as I'm concerned."

She looked like she understood, but she also brought up a few points I hadn't thought of before. "Ron, if you don't take the retest, a lot of people will say it was because you were afraid you would fail it."

"Not the people who know me," I answered. "Not the people who matter to me."

"You may be surprised," she said. "And hurt. Also, have you thought about what it would mean not to wrestle for a season? I know how much the practices and the matches mean to you. Is there anything you can think of that could replace them?"

That one hit home. I lived all year for wrestling season. I tried to imagine going through a winter without it, and I failed. "But do you think I should do something that I don't believe is right, just because it's the easy thing to do?" I asked her.

"You're going to have to decide for yourself," she told me. "I guess the important question is how much this moral position against drug testing means to you."

I was upstairs in my room trying to do some algebra homework when the doorbell rang. By the time I started down the stairs, my mother was already ushering Coach Brogan into our living room. Coach Brogan knew my mother a little bit from seeing her at my wrestling matches, but as I came down the stairs I sensed that he felt a tiny bit awkward about coming into our house at night. He had his hat in his hands, and when she motioned him to sit down in a chair, he nodded a thank-you and sat down very slowly and carefully. Maybe he was afraid his enormous frame would snap the chair into pieces if he sat down suddenly.

"Would you like some cake and coffee?" she asked him as I entered the room.

"No, thank you," he said. "I don't want to put you to any trouble."

"It's no trouble at all," my mom said with a smile. "It's a pleasure to have company."

"A small piece sounds terrific," he told her. "I . . . I still watch my weight very carefully. It comes from all my years in wrestling and football. It's silly, I know, but . . ."

"It's not silly at all," my mom told him. "I'll get you a small piece. Ron?" she asked.

"No, thanks, Mom," I told her automatically. "I'm in training." Coach Brogan looked at me quickly, as if he hoped that my words signaled a decision to keep wrestling. "Habit," I muttered. "I turn down food without even thinking about it."

"It's been a rough day," he said. "I've been thinking a lot."

"Me too," I told him. "I'm sorry to put you through all this."

There was a brief, awkward silence. Coach Brogan looked around our living room, searching for something to say. It was kind of funny—Coach Brogan was very graceful athletically, and in the wrestling room he

51

barked out orders with the complete confidence of an army officer, but in my living room he looked clumsy and uncomfortable. I saw his eyes examine the picture of my father in his army uniform, and it was almost as if I could hear the coach making a decision not to mention my dad. He looked at the little carved sculptures that my mother and I had brought back from our cross-country trip a few years ago. There were little statues of American Indians that we had bought at reservations; wooden nickels, dimes, and quarters that we had gotten in Las Vegas; and a small wooden whale from Fishermen's Wharf in San Francisco. Coach Brogan apparently couldn't think of anything to say, because his eyes swung over to my mom's big painting. He stared at it intently.

My mom has been painting for years, and this is her masterpiece. It's a painting of a summer lightning storm raging around Storm King Mountain at twilight. The mountain looms huge and dark, like an enormous, brooding face with heavy jowls and deep-set eyes. The lightning flickers around the grim colossus like a tangle of fiery hair.

"That's some painting," Coach Brogan murmured.

"My mom's masterpiece," I told him.

He looked at me quickly. "No kidding? It's . . . majestic."

My mother came back in the room with a tray of coffee and cake. She saw what we were looking at and smiled. "Please excuse any pieces of amateur art you may come across in this house, Mr. Brogan."

"Dan," he said. "Please call me Dan." Then he surprised me by saying, "It's wonderful. You seem like such a—happy woman. Where did such a gloomy picture come from?"

She took his question seriously. Her voice dropped down to a whisper, as her eyes climbed the mountain in her painting. "I spend a great deal of time living in the past—daydreaming backward rather than forward." Then she looked back at us and almost seemed embarrassed by what she had just said. "But that never does any good, does it? We must live in the present. And right now we have a problem."

"Yes, we do," Coach Brogan said. "You told your mother all about it?" he asked me. I nodded. "Believe me," he said to her, "I have one hundred percent confidence in Ron."

"Of course you do," she said, as if it was obvious.

"But a policy is a policy. Without passing a retest, he won't be allowed to wrestle this year. It would be a tragedy for him, for the team, for everyone. So, Ron"—and he paused for a long minute to look right at me—"I want to ask you to please take the retest. You took the test once . . . just take it again. Let's end this nightmare before it begins. Please."

They both looked at me.

"Isn't there any way I could wrestle without taking the test?" I asked Coach Brogan. "Is there some official I could talk to about my reasons for not wanting to take it? Is there some kind of appeal we can make?"

Coach Brogan looked sad and upset. "It's a new policy, and I'm sure the county board understands that it's going to be controversial. I could ask for some kind of special hearing, but I doubt—" He broke off and turned to my mother. "You care about him even

53

more than I do. Tell him he should just go ahead and take it."

"I raised my son to think for himself and stick up for his own beliefs," my mom said. "We both know Ron well enough to know that he doesn't give in to pressure—even from his own mother." Then she surprised me by saying, "But, Ron, if you want my opinion, I think you should take the retest and keep wrestling. I think you'll be happier."

Coach Brogan suddenly came alive, as if he had been floundering and my mom had unexpectedly thrown him a life preserver. "Listen to your mother—she knows what's best for you," he told me. "Nobody knows about this problem but the three of us. If you take the retest tomorrow, this whole thing will just fade away. But if you don't—" He paused as he searched for words and swallowed a forkful of cake. "You go to a small school. If you don't take that retest tomorrow, I'll have to tell the athletic director and the principal. This will get real messy. The news will be out before long, and it will spread like fire through dry tinder."

"I'm not afraid of what people will say," I told him. "Every kid at school knows I don't do drugs."

"Ron," he said, "I'm going to ask you a question that occurred to me tonight driving over here. I know you don't do drugs, but have you been to a party recently where other people were smoking pot?"

I shook my head.

"Just think," he said. "And maybe at such a party somebody near you was smoking and exhaling and you breathed some in? Or maybe somebody gave you a brownie to eat that tasted a little funny? It could have happened."

"I don't go to those kinds of parties," I told him. I stood up. "You're not beginning to doubt me, are you?"

He stood up too. "That test is supposed to be nearly infallible," he said slowly and clearly. "The samples are numbered and kept under security. There must be some logical explanation. I trust you, but I'd sure like to know why you tested positive. Now a retest would settle a lot of these questions once and for all. Ron, please . . . for me, for all the hours we've worked in the wrestling room . . ."

"I'll think about it," I promised him. "I'll let you know tomorrow morning. It's not an easy decision for me." I hurried up the stairs before I could weaken and make a promise to him right then and there. I wanted to think this over on my own.

Our house is so small that you can't help hearing a lot of what goes on in other rooms. I was kind of surprised that Coach Brogan didn't leave right away. I heard him downstairs talking to my mother about his days in college and pro football. I figured she enjoyed the company. We entertain guests very rarely, and Mom usually spends the evening reading.

As she walked him to the door, I heard Coach Brogan thanking her again for the cake. "An old bachelor like myself doesn't get to eat that kind of home cooking too often."

"Well, we'll have to have you over for dinner sometime," she told him.

"I'd be delighted," his voice answered, and then

there was the *thwack* of the heavy front door closing behind him.

I lay awake in bed that night, turning the problem over and over in my mind. I seemed to have two opposite and equally strong opinions on the same matter. I knew what I wanted to do: I wanted to take the retest and lead our wrestling team to the winning year Coach Brogan envisioned. And I knew what I had to do: I had to be true to myself and my beliefs and make a stand for what I felt was right.

As dawn broke, I made my decision. I had just about convinced myself to take the retest. My mind had constructed an ingenious line of argument to rationalize that taking the drug test was the right thing to do. I asked myself, Who would be hurt if I didn't take the test? Coach Brogan; my friends on the team; all the wrestling fans, including my mom, who came to our matches; and me. Next I asked myself, Who would be hurt if I did take the test? Again, I myself would be hurt because I would be selling out. But no one else would directly suffer. Surely it was more right, more moral, to choose the path that would not directly hurt the people I loved most. Surely, I told myself, in order to do right it was okay to take a test that I knew deep down was wrong for me to take.

The logic struck me as oddly familiar. I was thrown back to the night the police had picked me up and I had ridden in the backseat of the police car, shivering. And I had waited on the stool in the bare room beneath the bright lights, and in my dizziness had actually felt guilty. And Officer Garrison's words repeated themselves in my memory: *Sometimes when there's a lot on the line and you're trying to do the right thing, you have to kind of wink at the law a little bit.* And then I felt the same anger I had felt at the time, and I knew that those words were false and wrong.

COACH BROGAN WAS GALLANT in defeat. He agreed to contact the county board and set up an appeal as quickly as possible. "I understand your decision," he said, and his mixed emotions did strange things to his voice. "I'm not surprised by it. I even admire you for making it," he said. Then he paused, and the sadness made his firm features sag slightly with regret. "But I wish you'd picked another season to make a stand. I really thought we'd be getting another trophy in that case this year."

I told Stinker and Gorilla what I had decided, and soon the news was all over school. A lot of the guys on the wrestling team asked me about it, but once practice began, everyone was working too hard to waste breath on questions. I really enjoyed the sweat and the silence. Even the calisthenics were a pleasure to do. I barked out the repetitions faster than usual and threw in two extra sets of thirty push-ups. Groans were coming from all over the room. Suddenly, just before the last set, Coach Brogan tapped me on the shoulder. "Ron, come outside for a second."

I noticed that Mr. Ford, our high school's athletic director, was standing by the doorway. He was a tall man with a gaunt face. Gorilla took over leading the team in the last set of push-ups as I followed Coach Brogan and Mr. Ford out the door of the wrestling room.

Coach Brogan was angry. "I think you have no call to come in here and interrupt wrestling practice like this," he told Mr. Ford.

"I had no choice," Mr. Ford told him and turned to me. "Ron," he said, "according to the new county rules, I can't let you practice with the team."

That was a shock. Everything was happening so quickly. I examined his face and didn't see much sympathy. "Why not?" I asked him. "I'm in the best shape of anyone on the team. Ask Coach Brogan. I just did four sets of thirty push-ups, and I'm not even breathing hard."

"County rule," Mr. Ford said. "Every student who participates on a varsity athletic team must first pass a drug test. Participation includes practices and inter-school competitions. If I let you practice today, I would be violating the rule."

"Coach Brogan is trying to set up an appeal hearing with the county athletic board," I told him. "Shouldn't you assume that I'm innocent until they find me guilty?" My voice got a bit angrier. "C'mon, Mr. Ford,

59

you've known me for years. How about sticking up for someone you know?"

He didn't even blink. His long face, with its sharp chin and hollow cheeks, remained frozen in a refusal to argue the point. "The rule is the rule," he said. He took a step away and then turned back. "For what it's worth, I happen to believe in drug testing. The test is accurate. If it says you smoked pot, then you smoked pot. Chemical tests don't lie."

Coach Brogan and I stood there watching his black shoes step away down the corridor. "I have no choice," Coach Brogan mumbled.

"I know," I told him. "Any luck with the county board?"

"They're considering granting you a hearing," he told me. "I'll know in a day or two."

"Okay," I told him. "I'll work out on my own for a few days."

He went back into the wrestling room, and I stood for a while in the empty basement hallway. The reek of sweaty bodies and wrestling mats made the air heavy. I listened to the grunts and groans of my teammates and heard Gorilla barking out sets of sit-ups with his deep, deep voice. Then I headed home.

My mother put down her fork and said, "Tell me."

"Tell you what?" I asked her.

We were in the middle of dinner. I had spent the previous ten or fifteen minutes trying to wind bite-sized knots of spaghetti up on my fork and convey them to my mouth. I was failing miserably. Part of the reason was that I have always been absolutely incompetent at eating spaghetti. The strands slip off my fork faster than I can wind them on. The other reason I was eating so slowly was that I felt wretched.

Mom gave me a long look. She has piercing brown eyes that seem to dig deeper and deeper when they remain focused on one spot. Now they were focused on me. She has a kind face and a warm smile, but there are faint lines of worry and determination that occasionally harden the areas from her eyes to her chin. Tonight she looked worried. "Nobody eats spaghetti that poorly," she said. "Tell me."

We had spent so much time together that I understood her perfectly. "I just don't feel good," I mumbled. "May I be excused?"

"Are you sick?"

"No," I told her. "It's not that. It's just that things have been going on at school that really bother me."

"Like what?" she wanted to know.

"It's all a result of this drug test thing. Coach Brogan has set up a meeting with the county athletic board tomorrow morning, so maybe we can reach some kind of a compromise."

"You don't really want a compromise, do you?" I shook my head. "So what are you going to do?"

"I don't know," I told her.

She wound up a perfect forkful of spaghetti and popped it into her mouth. She was thinking hard. I let the silence drag on. "Would you like to talk to a lawyer?" she asked. "Get some legal advice?"

"We can't afford a lawyer," I told her.

My mom hates to be told that we can't afford something. When she married my father, fresh out of high school, she didn't have a skill. I guess she just planned to be a housewife. Then, when my father died, she took a job as a receptionist in a doctor's office. Slowly, over the years, she took classes and became a nurse, and as her qualifications improved, her salary got higher and higher. I know she did it all for me. She never wanted me to feel deprived. When one of my friends got a new baseball mitt or a bike, she would

62

take me out and buy me one too. And now she looked angry when I said we couldn't afford a lawyer. "We could at least afford a consultation," she pointed out.

"Please, drop it," I told her. "I don't want a lawyer. I don't want to make a big case out of this. I just want to be allowed to wrestle the way I've always been allowed to wrestle."

"But you don't want to give in and take the test? You would see that as a violation of your principles?"

"I've tried to convince myself to just shut up and take the damn test," I told her. I very rarely say *damn* at the dinner table, but tonight she let the word pass. "I used every argument I could think of on myself, but I just don't feel it's right."

She smiled a strange smile. "In some ways you're so much like your father," she said. "Once he made up his mind to do something, he could never change in the least little bit. He was always telling me to think for myself and not to let myself get pushed into things."

"Yeah, that's why he let himself get sent to Vietnam," I replied before I even knew what I was saying. "He really thought for himself on that one." The bitter sarcasm in my voice surprised me.

She slapped me hard and so fast I barely saw it coming. She hadn't hit me in years, and it took me a second to realize what had happened. She had her hand up as if she was going to strike me again, but I could tell that she was sort of frozen in surprise at what she had just done. My cheek burned where she had slapped me.

"Excuse me," I said, and got up from the table.

I was halfway to the kitchen door when she spoke.

Her tone was razor sharp. "You owe your father an apology."

"If he was here, I'd give him one," I told her.

"Shame," she said. Then she said, "You owe me one, too."

"For what?"

"For making me so angry I hit you."

I thought about it for a second. At first glance, it seemed like a strange reason to owe someone an apology. Then I saw the truth behind her words. I walked over, bent down, and kissed her on the forehead. "I'm sorry," I told her. "I guess I'm so mixed up I said something I shouldn't have. It's been one of the worst weeks of my life."

She nodded. She was crying, but in a very unusual way. Her face didn't soften—the tears trickled down her cheeks like raindrops. "Your father was a very wonderful man," she told me. "And you *are* very much like him."

"Maybe I am," I admitted in a whisper. "I didn't know him, so I don't know." I backed away slowly. "I'd better go upstairs and do my homework."

Once out of the kitchen, I sped through the hall and took the stairs two at a time. Soon I was up in my room with the door shut and my school books spread out on my desk. I channeled all my nervous energy into fierce concentration and finished three pages of math problem sets in about fifteen minutes. I tore through the week's chemistry chapter and learned nearly everything at first glance. My short-term memory works like that sometimes. I put my books away and sat there with my elbows up on my empty desk and the clock on the shelf ticking out a rhythm of passing seconds. *Tick, tick, tick, tick.*

I looked around the room. There were row upon row of sports trophies—sure, it had been nice to win them, but it would have been infinitely nicer to have won them with my father looking on. For the millionth time, I damned him for not being there.

There were doodads I had brought back from the trip I had taken across country with my mom. She had saved for the trip for two years, and we had planned it out on a big Rand McNally map on our kitchen table, and sure, it had been fun and interesting, but it would have been indescribably better to have taken the trip with my father at the steering wheel. For the millionth and first time, I damned him for not being there.

I slammed my hand down on my desk so hard that the wood surface trembled. Downstairs I could hear my mom clearing up the dinner dishes and loading them into the dishwasher. So she was a saint. So she was a martyr. So she could come home after long workdays and devote herself to me and to running our house. She could find satisfaction by looking backward at her slain hero of a husband and go on from day to day dreaming that in some way he was still with her. She could do all these things . . . but I couldn't. He hadn't been there for me, and I hated him for it.

I felt myself getting all tense the way I sometimes do when I think about my father, so I reached up for a book from the shelf above my desk. On that shelf I keep all my favorite American history books. There's Carl Sandburg's *Abraham Lincoln: The War Years,* and Samuel Eliot Morrison's *History of the American People,* and *The Writings and Speeches of Daniel Webster,* and an annotated copy of *The Federalist Papers,* and John F. Kennedy's *Profiles in Courage.*

I took *Profiles in Courage* down and skimmed through it, reading my favorite chapters. I read the one about how Senator Edmund G. Ross had knowingly wrecked his own promising political career by casting the crucial vote to acquit President Andrew Johnson in his impeachment trial before Congress. I glanced at the chapter about how Daniel Webster in a brilliant speech endorsed the Clay Compromise and by doing so doomed himself to years of hatred and condemnation by his former closest friends and admirers. He believed the Clay Compromise was the only way to save the Union, so he endorsed it, even though he understood the terrible personal consequences.

These were men I could admire. Ever since junior high school I had been reading about them and marveling at their ability to make tough decisions. I put the book down and thought about tomorrow morning's hearing. In many ways it had been the toughest decision I had had to make yet in my life, and I wondered if I would be able to justify it. Surely, I told myself, the question of how my decision would affect my own life and the team's success was secondary. The crucial question was: Did I believe some county athletic board could require young American citizens to take drug tests? Did they have the right to force me to give up a sample of my own body fluids? To me, the answer was no.

COACH BROGAN WAS more nervous than I was. "These will be the top athletic officials in the county," he said as we drove along. "Be respectful."

"I will," I promised him. I didn't know what sort of hearing I was going to get. Were they expecting me to make a speech? Was it going to be informal? Would they grill me with questions?

We turned into the parking lot of a large office building. Coach Brogan led the way to the fifth floor. Secretaries and administrators glanced at us, and I wondered if I had dressed formally enough. I was wearing a jacket and tie, neatly creased khaki pants, and newly polished brown loafers. Coach Brogan was wearing a formal dark gray suit. I tried to emulate his straight, almost military bearing.

A receptionist directed us down a hallway to a door

marked JOHNS COUNTY ATHLETIC ORGANIZATION. Coach Brogan looked at me and gave me a light punch on the shoulder for encouragement. I took a deep breath, opened the door, and walked inside.

It was a large conference room with four long tables connected end-to-end to form a hollow square. Three men in business suits were sitting along one side, talking. They all looked up as we entered. "Come in, come in," one of them said, standing up and hurrying over to us. He had silver hair and a gentle face and tone. "I'm Don Schiller, president of the county board." He shook Coach Brogan's hand and then mine, and for a man his age he had a surprisingly powerful handshake. "This is Bob Jenkins, vice-president, and this is Herb Green, our consultant on legal and policy questions. Please, sit."

We sat across from them. "I saw your final match last year against Igor," Mr. Schiller said to me. "You were both tremendous."

"Thanks," I said. "He was way better than me."

Mr. Schiller shook his head. "Not the way I saw it. You pushed him, and nobody else in the county even made him break a sweat. This year . . ."

"This year he's still the best in the county," I said. "Maybe the state."

Coach Brogan spoke for the first time. "Ron is being modest. He's been training all year, and he's in superb shape. This year it should be a great match. That's one of the reasons it's so important that Ron be allowed to wrestle this season."

Mr. Schiller smiled. "I agree," he said. "No one would like to see that match more than I would.

68

Which brings us to the problem that has created the need for this special hearing." He glanced down at some notes and then back up at me. "Ron," he said, "I'm going to ask Bob to give you a little background information about why we have installed the new drug testing program."

Bob Jenkins, the vice-president, was a hard man. I had seen him before, at meets and matches, and he had a reputation for always insisting on the letter of the law. He was completely bald and had thick black-rimmed glasses that he continually polished with a silk handkerchief. When he spoke he looked right at me, and he didn't show any sympathy or emotion at all.

"Drug tests are now being required by almost all major colleges and many high schools," he said. "The goal of drug testing is to protect student athletes. Athletes subject their bodies to unnaturally high levels of stress during practices and competitions. Different drugs weaken the body in different ways. The drug test we use can pick up nearly three hundred different drugs, from such common substances as marijuana and cocaine to drugs like steroids and barbiturates, which are much rarer on the high school level. In cases where a student tests positive, we recommend a program of drug education and rehabilitative counseling."

"I guess that's enough," Mr. Schiller cut him off. "But you should know, Ron, that we didn't implement this policy without a good deal of debate. The drug-related death of a football player at Cougar High last year was one of the deciding factors. We are responsible for the safety of high school athletics in this county, and we simply had to do something about a serious

69

and growing problem." He smiled at me. "Now, why don't you tell us your version of what's happened in the past few days."

The room got very quiet. I could feel them all looking at me, waiting. For a long minute my mind went blank and I couldn't think of anything to say. "You should know something about me," I told them. "I have a reputation at my high school for being the straightest guy around. I'm the only guy in school who wears his hair as short as Coach Brogan." They smiled at that. "My own girlfriend even thinks I'm much too straight." They smiled again, and Mr. Schiller chuckled.

"I've never tried a drug in my life—I've never even smoked a cigarette. I don't drink. I watch what I eat very carefully, I try not to stay up too late at night, and I don't watch much television. I'm a wrestler and my body is my chapel. I swear this to you."

"I've never seen a high school wrestler with so much discipline," Coach Brogan told them.

"You would seem like the last person in the world who wouldn't want to take a drug test," Mr. Schiller said.

"My hobby," I told him, "is reading American history. I love that stuff. Along with wrestling, it's my main interest. Someday I think I'd like to go into politics or constitutional law. My room is filled with books about people like Abraham Lincoln and Daniel Webster."

The three men from the county board were listening to me carefully. I couldn't tell from their faces if any of this was making sense to them.

70

"Anyway," I said, "I've read a lot about a citizen's right to privacy. His right not to have his phone tapped, or his house searched without a warrant, or his personal health record released to an insurance company. Since there is so much more access to information, preserving privacy is a real problem. And if common law says that a man's house is his castle, and the Fourth Amendment states that an American citizen can't be subjected to unreasonable search and seizure, then I think a person's own body must be even more fully protected. By insisting everybody take a drug test, you're really searching the inside of every athlete's body."

Bob Jenkins leaned forward, and his tone was curt. "But Ron, you've already taken one drug test."

"I took it against my better judgment," I told them. "And while I was being tested, I felt like I was doing something that was untrue to my own beliefs. I don't want to have that feeling again."

"But the fact is," Bob Jenkins said, "you failed that drug test. Now all of what you say about your beliefs and your rights is very impressive, but you took a test and you failed it."

They were all looking at me, waiting for me to respond. "I don't know what happened with that test," I told them. "I'm not an expert on drug testing, so I don't know what can go wrong. But I know myself. I know I've never smoked a joint or done a drug in my life."

Silence. I looked from one face to the next.

"A couple of weeks ago I had a bad experience," I told them. "The cops picked me up when I was out

71

jogging. I fit the description they had of a wanted criminal. Even our shoes seemed to match. It was really strange—I knew I hadn't done anything, but as that night wore on, I began to doubt myself. I actually began to feel guilty. The way I fit the description seemed too exact to be a mere coincidence. The police treated me like a criminal, and I began to feel like one."

I paused for breath. Mr. Schiller smiled encouragingly for me to finish. "Anyway, I'm kind of glad I had that experience because this time I don't doubt myself at all. I know I'm not guilty. I know I've never used drugs. And my family knows it, and my friends know it, and my teammates know it. Let me wrestle this year. I want to make Igor suffer a little."

Mr. Schiller cleared his throat. "Thank you," he said. "You speak well. Now please step outside for a few minutes so that we can discuss the matter. Then we'll let you know what we've decided."

I waited in the hallway with Coach Brogan. There was a water cooler out there, and we both sipped Dixie cups of ice water. The waiting soon got on my nerves. The *click, click, click* of the secretaries' typewriters chipped away at my self-control.

Mr. Schiller ushered us back into the room, and we sat down. I looked at their faces very carefully, but I couldn't tell what they had decided.

"I'm sorry, Ron," Mr. Schiller said. "If you want to wrestle this season, you're going to have to retake that test. We'd like to make an exception, but we just can't. A rule is a rule."

Coach Brogan stood up, and I stood up also. I

72

headed for the door and was halfway down the hall when Mr. Schiller's voice stopped me. "Ron," he said. I stopped. "Could I talk to you for a second?" I walked to meet him. "You're a very impressive young man," he said to me. "I want to give you a word of advice. Unofficially. Just between the two of us." He bent his head, and his voice came out in a sharp, hard whisper. "Don't be a fool. Take the test."

I looked up at him for a second, shook my head, and walked away.

It was a small creek fed by underground streams and fenced in by a crowd of willow trees along its banks. In the autumn, as the water got colder, the fish got more and more sluggish. This Saturday morning I was the first one to arrive. I rigged my line with a big bobber about six feet from the hook and then attached a few weights so the hook would dangle straight down. I put a worm on and made a long, arching cast. My bobber plunked down about thirty-five feet from shore, near the lily pads. It was as good a spot as any. I sat back on the bank and took a few deep breaths.

The air smelled sweet and damp. Water bugs turned cartwheels on the creek's glassy surface. A faint morning breeze made the willows whisper. Gorilla, Stinker, and I had been coming to the creek to fish for about ten years. I knew every large rock along the bank and every reed patch in the shallows, and just sitting there made me feel more relaxed than I had in days.

The bobber disappeared. I set the hook and instantly knew it was a bluegill, one that was too small to keep. The seven-inch fish put up the best fight it could, but I soon had it in my hands. I took the hook out and tossed it back, and the sunlight created a tiny rainbow on the bright scales of its back. It lingered for a second, unsure of itself, and then darted away. I rebaited the hook and threw it out to nearly the same spot as before.

Gorilla showed up about ten minutes later. He was wearing shorts and a sleeveless T-shirt, and his hairy legs and low-slung arms made him look even more like a gorilla than usual. "Anything?" he asked.

"Tossed one back," I answered. "Where's Stinker?"

Gorilla muttered something I didn't catch. He fixed his line, baited his hook, and threw it out by the big reed patch. He sat down next to me and breathed deeply. "Air smells good."

"No big fish today," I predicted. "Getting too cool."

"You can never tell about big fish," he grunted. Then he smiled at me and said, "I did a little night fishing last night. Landed a whopper."

I didn't get it.

"Mary Renardi. Took her down to the reservoir."

"You're kidding." I was surprised. Mary was a very big girl—she must have weighed 160 pounds at least. I hadn't known Gorilla was even interested in her. "Have a good time?"

"I know what you're thinking," Gorilla said. "That she's not pretty."

"Did I say that? I asked you if you had a good time."

"In fact, she's ugly."

"I don't think so at all," I told him. "She's just a big girl."

"She's got hips like a rhino," Gorilla told me with a smile. "But know what? I like her. I really do. I think we're gonna have fun together."

"That's great," I told him.

"She's got a great personality. Makes me laugh for hours."

"Yeah, she's a fun girl," I agreed.

"You really think she's that ugly, huh?" he asked.

"No, I honestly don't think she's ugly."

"C'mon, I can take it."

"Gorilla, she's fine."

"Level with me."

I let go. "Okay, she's ugly. She's fat and her face looks like it got run over by a tank. Satisfied?"

Gorilla smiled gratefully and gave his line a little tug. "I'm not that much to look at either," he said. "If I was a girl I'd probably look worse than her."

"If you were a gorilla, though, you'd really be in demand," I told him.

Suddenly his float jerked down, down, down, out of sight. He set the hook and let out a whoop. "Here comes lunch."

"Crappy?"

"Bass, baby, bass," he said, pulling and reeling.

I saw it in the water about fifteen feet away. It was

lunch all right, no doubt about it. Gorilla maneuvered it near the bank, and I netted it and scooped it onto dry land. The largemouth bass was fat and still full of fight. It took me a minute to untangle its thrashing body from the green scoop net and hoist it up. "Two pounds easy," I announced.

"Three," Gorilla said. "That one eats two-pounders."

I took the hook out, held the fish down on a flat rock, and clubbed it to death with one sharp blow on the back of its head. We hooked our stringer through its gills and lowered it back into the creek to stay fresh.

"Stinker's not gonna believe that one," I said. "Hey, where is he, anyway?"

"I don't think he's coming today," Gorilla said.

"What?"

Gorilla pretended to be concentrating on putting a new worm on his hook.

"Whaddya mean he's not coming?" It had always been Gorilla, Stinker, and me at the creek. For years.

"I think he had something to do this morning," Gorilla said.

I knew the truth then, and suddenly I had a bitter taste in my mouth and all down my throat, as if I had just thrown up. I looked at Gorilla closely, and he dodged my eyes. "Because of me?"

"Let it go, Ron," he said.

"Because of my decision not to take the test?"

"He didn't tell me his reasons."

"And he didn't even have the guts to come and tell me face-to-face?"

Gorilla made a long cast, and the bobber landed in almost exactly the same spot as it had before. He sat back down on the bank, his rod braced between his knees. "Let it go," he advised again. "Stinker'll get over it. Just don't push him."

"Me push him? I'm the one who's going through hell now. I'm the one who needs to find out who my real friends are."

Gorilla turned and looked at me, and I think that was the first time I ever noticed that his large forehead and deep eyes made him look somehow wise. "Stinker's really your friend," he told me. "He'd cut his arm off for you."

"Terrific," I said. We sat there in silence for ten or fifteen minutes, watching the bobbers and feeling Stinker's absence grow more and more tangible. When Gorilla, Stinker, and I fished as a threesome, we never had a dull moment. One of us was always doing something to spark the other two to laughter. Now, with only two of us, it was a completely different dynamic.

I heard his footsteps before I saw him. Stinker wasn't carrying a fishing rod, and he had a strange look on his face. Gorilla looked surprised to see him. "Hey, Stinker, what are you doing here? I thought you had something to do."

Stinker looked past him at me. "I was sitting home, and then I knew that not comin' today wasn't good enough. I wanted to tell you why."

Gorilla put down his rod. "Oh, come on," he said. "Let's not have this get too ugly. Come on." He put his hand on my shoulder.

I shrugged it off and walked up to face Stinker. "Okay, tell me why."

Stinker took a deep breath. His pinched face was red with anger. "I didn't come fishing today 'cause I'm mad at you. I want you to know that."

"Well, I'm glad you had the guts to tell me."

"Damn straight I have the guts to tell you," he said. "Our whole season's wrecked 'cause of you."

"Why are you mad at me?" I asked him, and my voice seemed to be getting a tiny bit louder with each exchange. "Because I failed the drug test? You think I smoked pot?"

"Don't be a jerk," Stinker said, and he was almost shouting. "I wouldn't be mad if you smoked pot and failed the test. I'm mad because I know you never smoked a joint in your life. If you took that retest, you'd pass it. But you won't because you want to be complicated." He spat out the last word, *complicated,* as if it had a rotten taste.

Somehow we had gotten closer and closer together each time one of us had spoken. Now we were only inches apart. This time when I spoke, my voice came out real low. "So if you don't want to come fishing with me, then I don't know if we're still friends."

"I don't either," he said.

"I don't think we are," I told him. "I like to be able to count on my friends."

"I feel the same way," he told me.

Gorilla's low voice sounded desperate. "Come on, guys, for pete's sake. We've been friends since we were kids. This is ridiculous. Come on."

Neither of us looked at him.

"Good luck fishing," Stinker said to me. "I'm gonna go now."

"Thanks," I said. "Anyway, I respect you for coming out here."

"I don't need your respect," he said, and his bitterness suddenly swelled past the danger point. I saw his fists clench, and I thought for sure he was going to swing. Instead, he turned and walked away down the path.

"Yeah, now I know why they call you Stinker," I called after him.

"Suck off," he shouted without turning and was soon lost among the willows.

I stood there for a while after he was gone, feeling incomplete. It felt like one of my arms or legs had just been cut off. Gorilla stood next to me, an anguished look on his face. "Let's go," he finally said.

"What?"

"Let's get out of here. Fishing isn't going to be any fun today."

"No," I agreed. "I guess it isn't."

"Let's go find Stinker and talk this out."

"If you want to be with Stinker, then go after him," I told him.

"Have you lost your mind?" Gorilla asked me. I didn't answer him. I sat back down on the bank and picked up my rod. "Well, I can't just sit here and fish like it was the good old days," Gorilla said.

"Then go," I told him.

He reeled in his line and took his rig apart. He

pulled in the bass. "Coming?" he asked me when he was ready to leave.

"No, I think I'll stay and do some fishing," I said.

He took a few steps up the path and then turned. "I'll call ya, Ron. I'll call ya tonight."

"Okay," I said.

Then he was gone, and I sat there all by myself, watching the red and white plastic bobber float on the smooth surface of the little creek. The breeze shushed itself so that the creek grew still and the willows hung straight down. I felt very much alone.

"WE'RE HAVING A GUEST over for dinner tonight,"
my mom told me.

"I know. I saw the good china. Who is it?"

"Dan Brogan," she said.

"Coach Brogan? Why is he coming over?"

She was hurrying around the kitchen, turning flames
down under pots and sampling sauces with spoons.
"Because I invited him," she said.

"Therapy for me?" I asked. She looked at me
quickly, smiled, and shook her head. "Romance?" I
guessed once more. She blushed, shook her head again,
and opened the door of the oven. The delectable smell
of roast turkey seeped out and filled the kitchen.
"Then I don't get it. Why is he coming over?"

"I thought it might make everyone's dinner more
enjoyable," she said finally.

"Everyone's?"

"He struck me as a very lonely man."

It was funny, but I had never thought of Coach Brogan in terms of his personal life before. At school he was always surrounded by kids. "Can I help?"

"You can help by keeping out of my way," she said, carrying a dirty pan toward the sink.

"Mom, you look very pretty tonight," I told her.

She stopped with the pan still steaming in her hand and looked at me quizzically. "What's that supposed to mean?"

"Nothing," I told her. "Except that you do." And she did. Beneath her apron she had on a light blue dress, and for some reason it made her look softer and more graceful than usual.

"Thank you," she said. Then she got busy again, and I headed upstairs to put on a clean shirt.

Coach Brogan arrived right on time. My mother met him at the door and welcomed him in. He was all dressed up in a jacket and tie, and he seemed more nervous and awkward than I had ever seen him. He came through the front door apologizing. "I wanted to bring something, but I didn't know what would be good. I thought of a bottle of wine, but Ron and I don't drink. . . ."

"You didn't have to bring anything," my mom told him.

He handed her a package. "Anyway, I brought some Swiss chocolate ice cream. I hope that's okay."

"It sounds delicious. Thank you," she told him.

He smiled at me, but it was an awkward moment because we hadn't seen each other that much in school lately. He had been busy with the wrestling team, and I tried to keep as far away from The Furnace as possible. "How ya doin', Ron?" he asked me.

"Fine," I said.

"You look like you're keeping yourself in good shape."

"I run on my own. Habit," I told him.

"But you've gained a little."

"Five pounds," I said.

"And high time he put some meat on those bones," my mother broke in. "Now why don't we move into the dining room. The turkey is almost ready."

Coach Brogan's eyes lit up. "If there's one thing I love, it's a good roast turkey."

"Then you should enjoy tonight's dinner," she told him with a smile. "Please, come in."

We walked into the dining room. The table looked beautiful with fine china and clean, folded dinner napkins and silver serving bowls. Our dining room is the largest room in the house, and it always seems empty when just my mom and I eat in it. On the other hand, with his six-foot-five-inch frame, Coach Brogan seemed too big for it. When he first sat down, he knocked his fork onto the floor, and when he bent over to pick it up, he nudged the table so that all the glasses on it shook. I wanted to tell him to take it easy, but I kept my mouth shut.

It was a splendid dinner. We had homemade clam chowder and a big garden salad with a sharp sesame and soy dressing, and then Mom brought out the turkey. It must have been at least a fourteen-pounder.

Mom had carved up one side of it, but she had left the other side intact so we could see what a big and beautiful bird it was. She served the turkey with pecan stuffing, fresh cranberry sauce, a deliciously rich brown gravy, and golden-brown roast potatoes.

"I don't know how you ever kept your weight down," Coach Brogan told me as he surveyed the feast.

"It wasn't easy," I agreed. "That's one good thing about not wrestling now. I eat what I want. Two helpings, or even three." I saw him wince at the idea of me eating three helpings. Coach Brogan had drilled dieting discipline into my mind. I knew he had a firm one-helping rule himself, even though his sports days were long behind him.

"Don't let it all go," he advised as we waited for my mother to finish loading the table with food and sit down. "You worked too hard to get there." He spoke to me, but his eyes watched my mother.

"I stopped by the bakery on the way home from school the other day." I confessed to him, trying to grab his full attention. "I had one of those cream-filled éclairs in the window. It was so good I had a second one. I used to walk by that bakery during wrestling season and turn my face away from the window so I wouldn't see the pastries."

"Don't do that." His face looked very sad. "It's poison."

My mom sat down at the table then, and Coach Brogan and I kept silent. She said a prayer that struck me as a little strange. "Oh, Lord," she said, "thank you for this food we are about to eat. And please help three lonely people to enjoy their dinner and learn from each other."

Coach Brogan looked at her as if he didn't quite understand and then said "Amen." I seconded the amen, and in another minute we were all helping ourselves to the different dishes.

The dinner conversation was polite and amiable, if a bit restrained. Coach Brogan never seemed to completely relax. He had a nervous habit of dabbing at his mouth with his napkin, which he must have repeated at least a dozen times during the course of the dinner. My mother was more animated than usual and told some funny stories about the crazy mix-ups that can happen at a doctor's office. I thought Coach Brogan laughed a little bit too loud at some of her anecdotes, but he's such a friendly man that even a fake laugh sounds warm coming out of his mouth. He responded with some hilarious stories about his days traveling with the Jets, and although some of what he said seemed a little bit in bad taste for dinner-table conversation, my mom and I both laughed.

Midway through the meal Coach Brogan turned to me and asked, "What have you been doing these days instead of wrestling practice?"

"Studying," I told him truthfully. "I've been reading a lot. And just kind of . . . hanging out."

"Maybe you should get a job," he said.

"Maybe I should," I agreed.

I wanted to stop talking about me and the way I spent my time.

"We're gonna need a student assistant in the athletic

office. To help out after school when all the coaches and teachers are busy. It wouldn't pay all that much, but . . . ."

"No, thank you," I told him.

"Ron, you should at least think about it," my mom said. "It would give you something to do."

My voice when I spoke was too loud for a dinner-table conversation. "Forget it, okay?" I lowered my voice. "I mean, it's torture for me just to walk by the athletic office and think about the wrestling team. I couldn't work there. Okay?"

"Okay, sorry," Coach Brogan said. And after that he didn't try to talk to me, but just joked with my mother. He had only one big helping, but I had three. The more Coach Brogan and my mom were having a good time, the more I felt like eating. I could sense the coach watching me as I reached for the stuffing plate and put another huge dollop of food on my plate.

"Best dinner I've had in years," Coach Brogan said as my mom cleared the table. "Need a hand?"

"You just sit right there and I'll bring some ice cream," she said. "I'm glad you enjoyed a little home cooking."

"Ruth," he said, "if you ever open a restaurant, I'll be your first and best customer." It was the first time he had called my mom by her first name.

She brought in the ice cream. Coach Brogan had half a scoop. He asked Mom about her painting and complimented her again on her picture of Storm King Mountain. She started talking about the difficulty she had in finding time to paint and about how she thought that if she had started earlier and had had better training, she would have liked to be an artist. It was news to me. During all the meals we had shared together, when I had talked about my wrestling and my grades and other stuff about school, she had never mentioned her artistic ambitions. She got kind of excited talking about it. I had three huge scoops of ice cream.

Then it was Coach Brogan's turn to surprise me. "It's so good to just have people around at dinner to talk to," he said. "I don't talk about my personal life much . . . but I'd like to tell you something. I got married seven years ago to a wonderful woman. But things just didn't work out." He looked my mom right in the eye, and his voice was full and frank and non-judgmental. "I guess after a while she started to find me dull. I don't like to go out that often. And she was a little too wild for me. She was running around a bit. The time came when it seemed best for the two of us to go our separate ways." He looked at me and smiled and then looked back at my mom. "Anyway, it's a great pleasure for me to have this kind of sit-down old-fashioned type dinner with two such decent and nice people. It sort of restores my faith."

My mother nodded. I didn't know what to say, so I just nodded too.

After a while I excused myself. I had a math quiz the next day that I had to study for. As I headed out of the dining room into the living room, I heard their conversation and laughter continue. Then I did a kind of crazy thing. I took the picture of my father down from the fireplace where it had always hung. I held it in my hands for a few seconds and studied it. Dad did look like me a lot. He had a crew cut, and he had the same strong, thick neck and goofy smile. Even our eyes were the same. The military uniform he was wearing fit him well. I took the photo over to the bookshelf and stuck it in next to the old photo albums of my childhood. I looked back at the living room wall—it seemed painfully bare. Then I hurried up the stairs.

I felt just a tiny bit dizzy, so I lay down on my bed. I could come up with no reason at all for having taken down the picture. I wondered for the first time in my life if I could be going insane. Seriously. I wondered if there were any standards you could judge yourself by to see if you were cracking up.

Even with my bedroom door closed, bursts of laughter occasionally floated up from the dining room. I wrapped my head in my pillow and tried not to think about anything at all.

KRISTENE'S BEDROOM WAS soft and feminine. She had a pink-and-white bedspread and red curtains. A dozen different kinds of stuffed animals turned her bed into a fuzzy little zoo. I had never seen a stuffed grizzly bear before. She had two well-worn beanbag chairs next to her stereo. The room smelled faintly of perfume.

I sat in one of the beanbag chairs trying my best to study the krebs cycle. Kris was lying on her bed wrestling with a chemistry book, and every few seconds her efforts at concentration would contort her body into weird positions, and her short skirt would slide up her legs. Her legs were much more interesting than the enzymatic reactions of aerobic organisms.

It was the first time I had ever been in her house, and I felt a little nervous. What if her mom came home and found us in her bedroom? It was a huge house. The downstairs floor had two fireplaces—one in the living room and one in the dining room. There were some beautiful original works of art on the living room wall, including a print by Miró and a sketch by Picasso. I was very impressed. Compared to my mom's painting of Storm King Mountain, a Miró and a Picasso seemed like a whole other league of art. In fact, this whole house was in a different league from my own.

"How's biology?" Kris asked me.

"Dull. How's chemistry?"

"Duller." She closed her book. "One more formula and my brain's going to ionize."

She lay on her back with her blonde hair spread out beneath her head. My eyes traced the whole side view of her body from nose to toes.

"I've been missing you," she said. "We haven't seen each other in a week."

"We talk every day in school," I told her.

"That's not the same."

"I've been . . . going through a hard time," I told her.

"I know you have."

"I needed to spend a few days by myself."

"That's where you're wrong," she told me. "You need comfort, not loneliness. You should have come to me."

"Whaddya wanna hear?" I asked her.

"Reggae," she answered. Kris always knew exactly what music she wanted. "There's a Jimmy Cliff tape on top of the pile."

I found the sound track from *The Harder They Come*

and popped it in. The Jamaican beat was soon dancing through the bedroom.

"Would you like a glass of wine?" Kris asked.

"You know I don't drink," I told her.

"I know, but would you like a drink anyway?"

I looked at her. She was smiling. "What does that mean?" I asked her.

"As far as I'm concerned, you could have a drink and still not drink. I mean, I won't tell anyone. There's some good French wine in the fridge. My mom and I drank half a bottle of it during dinner last night."

I decided not to push it, so I just shook my head and glanced back down at the biology book. I kind of wished someone would get on the krebs cycle and ride it out of my life forever.

"I'm all stiff from cheerleading practice," Kris announced.

I put down the biology book and looked at her. She smiled. "How about giving me a back rub?"

I got up and walked over to the bed. I sat down next to her and began to rub her back through the thick layer of her red sweater. "Does that feel good?" I asked.

"Higher," she commanded.

"High enough?"

"Unhh." It sounded like a muffled yes. "Harder."

I pushed harder. My fingers found pockets of tightness between her neck and her shoulder blades, and I tried to erase them with firm pressure.

"Here," she said, "this should help." She reached back and tugged off her sweater and the shirt beneath it. She lay down on her stomach, and her back

92

gleamed white under the ceiling light. I touched her smooth skin. It felt firm and warm. I moved my hands in long, sliding arcs over her back, and she purred. "Unhook my bra, and it won't get in your way," she told me. I undid the hooks.

"Who taught you how to do this?" she asked.

"Nobody."

"Well, you have the knack," she said. "You have strong hands."

"From wrestling." I moved down to her lower back, just above her hips. The skin was a tiny bit looser, like the soil of a valley below a mountain range. "What do we do if your mother comes home?"

"She won't."

"But if she does? And finds us in your bedroom?"

"My mother respects my privacy," Kris said. "She's got two boyfriends of her own, and when she brings them home I don't say anything."

"Two of them?"

"They know about each other," Kris told me. "It's not as if my mom's lying to them. Frankly, I don't think she's that serious about either of them."

"Feel good?" I asked her.

"Yes. Give me some karate chops. Little ones. Don't be too gentle. That's it."

The heels of my hands beat a steady tattoo of tiny karate chops up and down her back. I found myself thumping in time to the music, as if I were adding a new drumbeat to the Jimmy Cliff sound track.

"Good?" I asked her after a while.

"Great," she said. I stopped, and she lay there like a kitten that has been stroked and stroked. Finally she said, "Take off your shirt and lie down, and I'll give you one."

I took off my shirt. When I raised my shirt over my eyes, she was sitting up on the bed next to me, and she hadn't put her top back on. My eyes were drawn to her fine, firm breasts. "Lie down," she said. "And try to relax."

I lay down. The clean, flowery smell of her pink bedspread crept into my nose and mouth. I tried to relax, but it wasn't easy. She knelt with her legs on either side of me, so that her knees and thighs sometimes brushed my ribs. Her warm little hands began at my neck and gently traced the ridges of my back all the way down.

"You have an unbelievable body," she said. "Your back has muscles on top of muscles."

"They're all turning to flab," I told her.

"Doesn't look like it." Then she began to press and knead up and down my back, and she really seemed to know what she was doing. I felt her thumbs seek out tense spots and probe them with constant pressure at different angles until they relaxed. Once she stopped massaging and bent over me to kiss the back of my neck. Her breasts rested deliciously on my shoulder blades. Her breath blew like a furnace on the back of my neck and ear.

"Okay if I apply a little pressure in a sensitive area?" she asked, massaging again.

"Go ahead," I said. "You won't hurt me."

But I had misunderstood her. Instead of pressing down on my back, she spoke, choosing her words very

94

carefully. "Everyone at school keeps asking me if you're crazy."

"What do you tell them?"

Her hands were now whisking lightly up and down my spine, punctuating her words with an occasional exclamation mark of pressure. "I tell them you're very complicated," she said, and it struck me that she used the same word Stinker had spat out at me.

"In what way do you think I'm complicated?" I asked.

She was silent for a few seconds. Her hands leapfrogged around on my lower back. "You know, people actually believe that you're sitting out the wrestling season because you're opposed to drug testing."

"Well, I am," I told her.

She gave a little laugh. "Like I said before, as far as I'm concerned, you can drink wine with me and still tell everyone that you don't drink at all. I want you to trust me like that." Her voice tapered down to a whisper. "If you smoked a little pot once or twice, it wouldn't make me think any less of your character."

I rolled her off. I half sat up, and she lay down next to me sideways. We were looking right into each other's eyes. "Is that what you think?" I asked her.

"I don't think it matters at all," she said, reaching out to comb my chest hair with the fingers of her right hand. "I don't think chemical tests lie very often. I mean, I've spent the last two days studying chemistry, and it seems like a pretty exact science."

"I can't have a girlfriend who doesn't trust me," I said.

"Would you rather I lied?" she asked.

I sat up and began to put on my shirt.

"Ron." She reached up and pulled me back down to the bed. She moved closer, so that we were both lying on our sides right up against each other. "Like I said before, it doesn't matter. You really don't care about drug testing any more than I do. Come on. I think I understand you a little bit."

"I don't know what you're talking about," I told her. "And I think I'm going to go now."

This time when I sat up she didn't try to restrain me. "Oh, come on," she said. "Do you expect me to believe that you're taking a big moral stand just for the sake of the issue? I mean, surely the season is more important than the issue."

"Read about the career of Muhammad Ali," I advised her as I finished buttoning my shirt. "He was the best boxer in history. The fastest. The flashiest. The best footwork. When he beat Liston the second time, he was still only twenty-three. His career looked absolutely golden. With each fight he seemed to get even better.

"Then they drafted him. He would never have seen combat, and everyone knew it. He would have spent his military days boxing exhibitions and living well, and in a few short years he would have been back as a pro. Instead he made a stand. He said, 'I ain't got nothing against the Vietcong.' And he was willing to sit out for years—the best years of his career—as his case went all the way up to the Supreme Court. People do take moral stands and give things up," I told her, "if they think an issue is important enough."

She sat up next to me. "Interesting choice of an example," she said. "Muhammad Ali. Vietnam. That's what this is all about. Not drug testing. Why don't you admit it to yourself? You're . . . striking out at your father by hurting yourself."

"That's ridiculous," I told her. "You're just trying to sound smart." The anger in my voice scared me.

"You were just waiting for a chance to come along to take a stand," she continued. "It could have been drug testing or it could have been anything else. You just had to show how much better and stronger you are than your father. I don't understand it completely, but it's because he went off to fight. And you think he did it without thinking. So you're going to show the whole world that you're better than he was. You're capable of taking a stand."

I rushed toward the door. I didn't want to hit her, and I knew I was going to if I stayed in that room a second longer. The door was hard to open, and I nearly yanked it off its hinges.

"So who's the next one you'll cut away?" she called at my back. "Your mother? Isn't she the only one you have left?"

I ripped the door open and fled down the carpeted stairs.

I TOOK IT out on Igor.

I had built my own version of The Furnace in our tiny basement to work out in when the school weight room was closed for the summer. It was a small space—about twelve feet long by seven feet high—with our house's old water boiler tank on one side and a gray stone wall on the other. There were no windows in our basement, and the only illumination came from a single naked light bulb, which I turned on by yanking a rope that dangled down from the ceiling.

I would go down to the basement room after school and work out for two hours till my mom came home. Sometimes when I'd have trouble sleeping, I'd go back down late at night when my mom was asleep and work out for another hour.

There was a chin-up bar that I'd mounted between

two thick wooden pillars. I could do sixty chin-ups before my arms began to sing out in pain. After my workouts I usually tried to do fifty or sixty pull-ups, and I'd often finish with five one-handed chin-ups, growling and sweating as I slowly lifted and lowered my body. On the wall behind the chin-up bar, I had tacked up a photograph from the newspaper of Igor getting the county championship trophy. I saw the photograph each time I went up and each time I came down. On the final one-handed chin-ups, when my arm felt so tired that I wanted to give up, I concentrated on that picture and used my hatred of Igor as the fuel to keep my body moving.

There was a very old and slightly shaky bench press, which I'd bought for eighty dollars at a church rummage sale. It was sturdy enough to work out on, but I never lifted my maximum for fear my arms would give out or the bench would collapse and there would be nobody down here to pull the bar off. I had heard of lifters being choked to death by the bar in such situations. I did sets of fifteen, lifting two hundred and thirty pounds in smooth, rhythmic motions while I concentrated on breathing evenly and putting my legs and back into the lift. And always before my eyes was the image of Igor standing over me, snarling. Sometimes I would imagine he was pinning me to the mat, and my arms would shoot the bar upward to throw off his specter and escape.

I had a jump rope. I would skip rope for long periods of time, drifting off into my own daydreams so that the only sound from the outside world was the *whisk, whisk, whisk* of the rope touching the basement floor. I

99

could do tricks with the rope by crossing my hands or alternating feet.

Last of all, I'd hit the heavy bag. I'd saved for it for over a year on my old newspaper route, and after I'd bought it, I spent months figuring out a safe way to hang it from the ceiling. Heavy bags weigh a lot, and the iron support I had finally put up to hang it from was now bent down several inches in the middle. I would assault that bag with a vengeance, hooking into it with lefts and rights and then thudding in combinations until my arms felt too heavy for me to keep punching. Then I'd imagine it was Igor in front of me instead of the bag, and he was sneering at me the way he'd sneered when he'd pinned me last year in the final period of our county championship match. My eyes would burn and my blood would start pumping and I'd move in with ten or fifteen more short, hard punches that would make the heavy bag whimper in protest.

I walked around all day waiting for the time when I could disappear down into that basement room and lose myself in two hours of fury. I was getting straight A's in all my classes, but I stopped answering questions or arguing with my classmates. I just didn't care enough to try to impress a teacher or argue with a bad answer, even if I knew someone had said something that was totally wrong. The only reason I continued to do so well in my classes was that I was having a lot of trouble sleeping. I often got out of bed at one or two in the morning and studied till dawn just to fill up the empty hours.

Insomnia is very odd. The more you think about

trying to fall asleep, the less chance there is that you will actually be able to do it. I had never had any trouble sleeping before, but now I went through a period when I'd be lucky if I got three or four hours. I would lie awake with my eyes closed, and thoughts of Stinker and Kris and Igor would whirl back and forth through my mind. I would turn over on my stomach or switch to my side or bunch up the pillows or hurl them onto the floor—it didn't matter; from any direction my mind was too troubled to slip into the sweet release of sleep.

After several weeks of this, I found myself walking to the gym to watch our wrestling team get humiliated by Northside Tech. Igor is the captain of Northside. They're not in our league, so we don't always wrestle them in regular season matches, but this year they were on our schedule. Before the season started, the newspapers predicted our two teams would be pretty evenly matched, but things had changed since then.

I wasn't planning to go to the match, but after dinner that night I suddenly knew that I had to go and see it for myself. It was a bitterly cold night, one of the first real freezers of winter. As I walked along High Street alone, the teeth of night wind chomped frostbite across my nose, cheeks, and forehead. It was cold enough to be snowing, but not a flake fell. I kind of enjoyed the sting of the wind and the ache of the winter chill.

The gym was nearly full for the big match. I arrived late and sat by myself up near the very top of the side bleachers. Thank God no one was dumb enough to try to sit near me. I could feel about two thousand eyes flick across my face as people noticed me and pointed me out to their friends. Even the guys on the Northside team spotted me. I saw one of them point, and then everyone on the bench looked over. The only guy who didn't bother looking was Igor.

It was a rout. Our team won only two of the matches. Northside Tech looked stronger and quicker and much meaner. Stinker Williams was slammed down so hard he got a bad nosebleed and couldn't continue. Another of our wrestlers was taking such a beating he seemed to let himself get pinned just to escape further punishment. And then it was Igor's turn.

I was surprised that Carl Stoner, with whom I had had the fight, had been able to lose ten pounds and move down to take my slot. He got out to the mat first, and I could tell he was doing his very best to look confident and unafraid. But I knew he was secretly quaking in his shoes, and I thought it was pretty obvious.

There must have been some Northside Tech fans there because Igor seemed to get a few cheers mixed in with the boos when he stepped onto the mat. I felt a rush of blood that made me dizzy. There he was. Igor. In my gym. And I had to sit on the bench and watch him wrestle somebody else. I think a few dozen people turned to look at me when Igor stepped onto the mat, as if they too felt I should be down there facing him.

I guess I should explain that wrestling is the loneliest and most solitary of all high school sports. Team sports like baseball and football and soccer are not nearly as intense because you have eight or nine or ten other guys to share the credit or the blame with. The other solo sports, like singles tennis, are played in a friendly atmosphere. There are always lots of smiles and cheers, and the players often exchange small talk and gestures of mutual respect.

In wrestling, it's *mano a mano.* The guy you're fighting doesn't only want to beat you—he wants to pin you in the shortest time possible. He wants to flip you over on your back and keep you there in front of a crowd of your friends and classmates. It's more than losing a match, and it's more than being humiliated—it's like losing all your pride in two seconds.

I should know about this, since I've pinned lots of people. I love to pin. I love it when you have a guy all tied up and he's trying desperately to keep his shoulders up, thrashing about like a bird, and you just grind him into the mat for the win. I like to feel that moment when he knows it's over and gives up, and the release of pride and will that makes his body slump when the ref slaps the mat to announce the pin. And, of course, I absolutely hate being pinned myself.

I've only been pinned twice in my whole high school career. Both times I was pinned by Igor in the county tournament with hundreds of people watching. The first time I was only a freshman and didn't really expect to win, so it wasn't too bad. I couldn't eat for two days afterward. But I recovered pretty quickly. The second time was nasty. Igor got me on my back early in the third period, and for minute after minute I hung on, bridging my back up and turning first one shoulder and then the other and putting every ounce of strength I had into the effort of keeping my shoulders off the mat.

I remember how it felt to try to resist the tremendous pressure of his arms and how his weight was always perfectly positioned, always digging into my remaining strength. Igor had horrible sour breath, and each time he exhaled, the stink from his mouth would surround me like a poisonous cloud. Believe me—every few seconds Igor would make a sound in his throat that sounded like a wolf's growl. He used every part of his body to force me down: his head, his shoulders, his knees, his feet.

And then I had finally yielded to the pressure and heard the ref slap the mat and the crowd roar. I felt the pride and confidence I had in my own fighting ability drain out of my body till I was so weak I could barely stand up. Usually the winner shakes the loser's hand, but Igor was sneering down at me with almost savage glee. His eyes looked narrow like a hungry dog's, his teeth gleamed in the light of the gym, and the muscles up and down his body stood out in angry definition. It was a sight that had kept me sleepless for weeks afterward, and that had driven me to train all summer to get even.

And now I saw Igor on a wrestling mat again. He looked even more ferocious than he had last year. His body rippled from head to foot with muscles. His oddly misshapen head was shaved bald, and there seemed to be ridges of muscle on his cranium. Igor's weird looks helped make him so savage—he scared away a lot of people and had very few friends. Even his wrestling teammates kept their distance. Maybe it was that loneliness that fired his temper. He seemed to be able to walk without having to lift his feet off the floor. Just by watching him glide to the center of the wrestling circle, you could tell that he had tremendous balance.

The match started, and Igor shot right in for a leg. Carl Stoner was experienced and fast and strong, but Igor had one of his legs almost instantly and in another instant had whirled around behind him for control. Carl tried to escape, but Igor tripped him down to the mat and then began prying him onto his back. It was amazing to watch. Carl was a senior and knew exactly what he should do to resist, but Igor simply destroyed him. His arms heaved and bent Carl as he grasped for leverage, and within about thirty seconds Igor had a perfect cradle hold. He cradled Carl onto his back, and the ref slapped the mat. It was over. The time of the match was about forty or fifty seconds. The gym was dead silent as Igor stood up and raised his hand. It was awesome and it was frightening.

Gorilla won his match on points, but our team went down to a very one-sided defeat. I couldn't believe this was the team I had practiced and wrestled with for two years. Except for Gorilla, there was no spark at all.

I sat there after the final match because I wanted to give everyone a chance to get out before me. I didn't want to face questions or anger or sympathy. When the gym was completely empty, I walked down the bleachers and headed out. I hurried through the exit and turned into the parking lot. There were more people hanging around there than I had figured on, so I put my head down and began to walk fast. Then I heard a voice that stopped me in my tracks. "Hey, you. Ron Woods."

105

I turned around. "Igor," I said. He had followed me out into the parking lot. He walked a few steps closer. A couple of people saw us and began to draw near, but Igor and I were looking right at each other. It was as if we were alone.

"You got more brains than I thought you had," he said. His low, low voice rumbled through the cold night air. "I heard the reason you're not wrestling this season is because you failed a drug test. But you don't take drugs, do you?"

I didn't say anything. He read the answer in my eyes.

"Yeah, you don't seem like you would. You didn't wrestle this season because you were afraid. You knew what I'd do to you. That guy they put out there instead of you tonight was garbage—I crumpled him up and threw him away. But you I would have killed. Really killed."

I kept my silence. Our eyes were locked in furious hatred.

"Know why?" he asked. "Because I read in some papers that you had a chance against me this year. Some guy even said you might beat me this year." He gave a laugh that didn't contain any humor at all.

"I would have given you a good fight," I said.

He became yet angrier. He stepped another few feet closer so that we were only a yard apart. Around us, I was vaguely conscious of a ring of people watching and listening. "You think so?" he asked. "Then it's funny that you didn't wrestle this year. I've been asking a lot of questions about you. I know some people at your school. I was curious."

106

He moved still closer. Now we were only six inches apart. I could smell his sour breath. Instinctively, I moved my legs apart to balance my weight evenly. My fists had been clenched during the whole conversation.

"I hear you don't have a father," he said to me. "I hear you were raised by your momma. So no wonder you weren't man enough to wrestle me this year. It takes a man to raise a man. You were raised by a woman and you're a little momma's boy. . . ."

I swung at his chin, but he ducked back with lightning speed and then crashed a right hand into my chest. Even through the padding of my winter jacket, it knocked the air from my lungs. Then he dove in, and I took the force of his charge and tried to twist him into the ground, and a second later we were on the black tarmac of the parking lot, exchanging punches and trying to get on top. It was a war. I landed a few bombs, but Igor got a grip on my jacket and used it to climb on top. He got off two or three clean shots at my face before Coach Brogan pulled him off. His own coach and a couple of guys from his wrestling team pulled him back, but as I struggled to my feet he lurched forward. I think he must have dragged eight guys a couple of feet. His eyes were twin spearpoints of hatred.

"Momma's boy," he snarled. "I cut you up. Run on home."

I WAS DOWN IN my basement, attacking the heavy bag, when I heard the door open and someone start down the stairs. I knew my mom's footsteps, and this was someone different. These were footsteps that made the old wooden stairs shudder and shake. "Hey, Ron," Gorilla called. "Okay if I come down?"

Before I could answer, he had reached the bottom step and stood in my little version of The Furnace. For a second I felt his eyes on my face, examining the cuts above my eye and across the bridge of my nose. Then, quickly, he looked up at me and smiled his wise and friendly gorilla grin.

"What are you doing here?" I asked him.

"Missed ya in school for a few days," he said. Then lower, "You don't return my phone calls so I thought

108

I'd better come over in person. See how you are mending."

"My mom let you in?"

"Sure she did. And she told me where you were. It's kind of late to be working out on a heavy bag, isn't it?"

I didn't say anything, but I hit the bag with a tremendous right-hand punch.

Gorilla walked to the chin-up bar and looked at the picture of Igor. He did a chin-up and his eyes stayed on the picture, exactly as mine always did. "This Igor is one ugly sucker," Gorilla muttered. "Ugly and mean."

"So why are you here?" I asked him.

"Because it's been snowing for four hours. It's not much fun to go tobogganing alone."

I hit the bag with two lefts and a right. "Go alone," I said. "I don't feel like it tonight."

Gorilla came over and grabbed the bag in his huge arms to stop it from swinging. "Come on, Ron," he said. "There's no one else going. Not Stinker or Kris or anyone from school. Just me. Come on. There's got to be at least six inches of new snow on the ground."

There was a long silence. I looked at Gorilla carefully. His wise, slightly simian face implored me with a hopeful grin. "You sure there's no one else waiting upstairs?" I asked him.

Now his grin was a smile. "Just me. Come on, let's go."

I put on the warmest winter clothes I had. On the outside I wore a green ski coat, jeans, thick gloves, and fur-lined boots. On the inside I wore long johns and

109

heavy woolen socks. Finally I came down the stairs, all bundled up. "Okay," I told him, "let's go."

It was snowing in thick sheets of whiteness. I could see only about twenty feet ahead. The snow was already nearly a foot deep in places, and from the look of it, would keep falling all night. There probably wouldn't be any school for a few days. That was fine with me. I wasn't planning on going back to school till my cuts healed.

"So what have you been doing with yourself?" Gorilla asked as we headed for the golf course.

"Homework on my own," I muttered. "And working out."

"All day?"

"I watch TV. And I've been reading a lot."

He was towing the toboggan behind him. We had had some wild times over the years with that toboggan. Two guys could steer it, but only with a little skill and a lot of luck. We had had hundreds of close calls.

It was a fun walk to the golf course. The town lay asleep beneath a blanket of gleaming snow. It seemed like a patchwork quilt as the moonlight stitched squares of lawn and pavement and woodland together. The streets were absolutely silent and deserted except for two large dogs, who ran out to us at the corner of Pine and Ames and began chasing each other, barking and yelping.

"Are you still going with Mary Renardi?" I asked Gorilla as we neared the golf course.

"Sure am," he replied happily. "Things have been great."

"I'm glad for you," I told him. "Really."

"Funny thing is, I knew she wanted to go out with me for two years, but I never gave it a chance before." Gorilla sounded thoughtful. "I knew that she wasn't beautiful, and I thought somehow I should be able to do better. I cared too much about what other people thought. Since we've been going out, it's been pure happiness." He stopped walking. We were half a block from the golf course. "I guess I've learned that you can turn your life into whatever you want it to be. You can build your own heaven." He looked right at me. "Or your own hell."

"Spare me the philosophy," I told him. "I came here for the sledding."

He nodded. "Okay," he said. "Only we all kind of miss joking around with you. Me, Stinker, Kris, the guys on the team . . . It's like you've become a different person. Kris told me you don't even return her phone calls."

I helped him tow the toboggan up the long slope. The huge open space of the golf course stretched all around us like a vast white sea. The tall drifts reared up like waves, and the narrow stream beds dropped down suddenly like deep troughs.

It was a half-mile hike up to the top of the slope. We saw one guy skiing along the fifteenth fairway, using his poles to push himself along the flat sections. The snow was coming down in a silent cascade of thick, wet flakes. Several times I wiped a thin layer of melting snow off my forehead.

We reached the top of the slope. "Front or back?" Gorilla asked. I took the front, and Gorilla got on behind me. We didn't push off right away, but spent a

111

few seconds looking down the fairly steep slope, picking out a rough course. We would try to steer left of the frozen lake and thread our way between the pine trees that divide the tenth and eleventh fairways. Then we'd be on the steepest part of the slope, and it would be up to me to spot the creek beds.

The toboggan started slowly, but after a few seconds we were whizzing along at a terrific speed. We skimmed the left bank of the frozen lake, and a few times the toboggan skidded along ice patches. Then we were on snow again, and as we flew forward and down, I searched for the path through the pine trees. "Right, right," I shouted to Gorilla, and then we were in among the trees, which bristled and bent to block our way like a group of angry ghosts. We almost hit two trees but were able to throw our weight in the right direction to avert disaster. Then the last tree gave way, and we were on the steepest part of the slope.

"Call out the streambeds," I heard Gorilla shout from behind me.

"I can barely see," I shouted back.

Our toboggan flew faster and faster on the fresh powder, till it really seemed to have taken wing and left the ground far behind. Ahead I saw a snake of shadow and screamed, "Left, left!" Somehow we missed the first streambed. I split the next two perfectly, but I knew that somewhere out ahead of us lay the stream that twists and winds the length of the bottom of the course. There are places where the stream's banks are so close to the bed that you can sled right over them and keep going. There are also places where the stream bed drops down ten or fifteen feet below the level of the course.

"See it?" Gorilla shouted.

"Not yet."

The wood of the toboggan sped soundlessly down the steep slope. The flakes of snow whirled by us, occasionally getting in my eyes and mouth. I tried to keep a sharp lookout, but it was hard to see anything.

And then it was right in front of us, about forty feet dead ahead. We were speeding toward the deepest part of the streambed. "Left, left!" I yelled, and the toboggan responded to our frantic efforts, but I knew we wouldn't make it in time. The abyss of streambed got closer and closer. "Bail out, bail out," I shouted at the last possible second and jumped off the toboggan. I flew forward through the air about three feet, and my momentum made me roll over the lip of the bank and down, down, down into the streambed. I went with the roll and finally came to rest in a patch of fresh snow. I lay there for a second, taking inventory. My body felt okay—nothing was broken or twisted. I stood up and let out a loud rebel yell. *"Ye-ee-ee-hah."*

"Stop screeching and help me up," I heard a muffled voice say from very close. I looked over and started laughing. Gorilla had been thrown into a deep drift. He was still half buried. He must have plowed into the drift headfirst. As I watched, he struggled to his feet and let out a loud rebel yell in return. *"Ye-ee-ee-hah."*

Then we both started laughing and throwing air punches at each other to celebrate because it had been

113

one of our best and most dangerous wipeouts ever.

"You okay?" I asked him as we started the search for the toboggan.

"Anybody ever teach you your right from your left?" he grunted. "You steered us into the deepest spot on the whole golf course."

"I wanted to see if you could take it," I told him.

"I can take it," he said, brushing snow out of his ears. "I just don't like it."

We found the toboggan stuck safely in a drift and made several more runs. None of the other runs was quite as much fun or as dangerous as the first one, but all in all it was one of the best sledding nights we had ever had.

"Thanks for dragging me out of the house tonight," I told him as we headed home. "I needed it. I've been thinking too much lately."

"I wish I could do more to help you," he said. "It's like you're taking a trip, and if I knew where you were going, maybe I could help you get there."

"I think I gotta ride this one out by myself," I told him.

"There's one thing that really bothers me, though," he said.

We turned onto Sylvan. The snow was so deep we didn't lift our feet completely out of it when we walked. The house lights were either off or hidden by the snow, so that the only lights I could see were the streetlights, glowing at fifty-yard intervals like a string of winter moons.

"What's bothering you?" I finally asked him.

He slowed down. "I don't mean to boast, but I've

114

already been offered two full scholarships. To good colleges. Not great ones, but good ones."

"Congratulations," I told him. "Really."

"No, that's not why I'm telling you. It's just that . . . if I could get two full scholarship offers with my wrestling talent and test scores and B average, I bet you could get twenty. I bet the Ivy League would come knocking on your door."

"Maybe not," I said.

"You've got the highest average in your class," he said. "Straight A's, unless you've screwed it up. There are half a dozen teachers who think you're one of the best students they've ever had. And when it comes to history, I hear Mr. Pilkington says he should sit down and just let you teach the class."

"He never said that—" I began to object, but Gorilla cut me off.

"I hate to see you throw it all away," he said. "Or most of it, anyway. Your mom has worked pretty hard to get you where you are. A full wrestling scholarship to college would take a lot of weight off her shoulders. Otherwise . . ."

We reached my house. "Thanks for thinking about me," I told him. "And about my mother. But we'll be okay. Wanna stop in for hot chocolate or something?"

Gorilla looked sad. "I gotta get home," he said. "Mary calls every night at eleven."

"To say good night?" I asked.

"And to check up on me. She's a sweetheart, but she doesn't completely trust me yet."

"She should," I told him and then walked up the path toward my house.

THE SNOW STOPPED and the streets were plowed, and after two snow days, school started up again. My cuts had healed a little bit. I returned to school, but I only stayed for the shortest possible period of time each day. As soon as my last class was over, I trudged home through the snow alone. I had never spent so much time alone before, and I noticed that it changed my personality in certain ways. I didn't have nearly as much energy as I used to have. I found myself dwelling on the past instead of enjoying the present or thinking about the future. I was far more observant of little things than I had been before, and in school I began to construct imaginary lives for the kids I saw every day but didn't know very well.

At home I was lazy. I kept up my workouts and did my homework, but I seemed to spend more and more time in front of the television set. I no longer had to check the TV guide to know what shows were on at any hour of the afternoon or evening. I found that the very best shows for turning off my mind were the game shows. I could watch them flow, one into the other, for hour after hour without feeling bored or restless. Such idiotic programs were similar, comfortable, and very numbing.

On a clear Sunday about a week after the snowstorm, I came up from my afternoon workout to find my mom writing down some directions on how I should heat up my own dinner. She had cut off some slabs of meat loaf, wrapped them in silver foil, and put them in the fridge. According to her notes, I should open a can of string beans and heat them for a few minutes, and there was fresh fruit in a bowl on the dining room table if I wanted dessert.

"What are you doing for dinner?" I asked her.

"Mr. Brogan—I mean Dan—is taking me out for dinner." She managed to say it without sounding embarrassed or nervous.

"You mean . . . you're going on a dinner date with my wrestling coach?"

"Yes," she said. Her face was suddenly set with decision, and her voice was firm and forthright. "Yes, that's exactly what I mean. And now I have to go upstairs and get ready. Are the directions clear?"

"They're clear," I told her. "Only I don't think I'll want any dinner tonight. I'm not hungry."

She looked at me hard. "Suit yourself," she said. "It's there if you want it."

She headed upstairs to dress. I sat down on the

couch and turned on the television. We have a remote control, so I could sit on the couch and switch the power on and change channels without ever getting up. I could hear her hurrying around upstairs between her bedroom and the bathroom.

The doorbell rang right at seven o'clock. I heard my mom coming down the stairs to answer it, so I didn't bother to get up. Mom's voice was bright and happy: "Hello, Dan, come in, come in, I'm almost ready." There was a brief pause. "Oh, thank you. They're beautiful. You shouldn't have."

I turned at this. Coach Brogan was standing in the hallway with a bouquet of a dozen long-stemmed red roses in his hand. "I wanted to," he said.

I had to admit Mom and Coach Brogan made a good-looking couple. He handed her the flowers, and she took them and smelled them and smiled. "I'll go put these in water, and I'll be ready in two minutes," my mom told him. She hurried with the flowers into the kitchen.

Coach Brogan walked into the living room so that he stood behind me. I didn't turn to look at him. "Hey, Ron," he said. "How are ya doing?"

"Fine," I answered. I kept watching TV.

"How's it going in school? Classes okay?"

"Fine."

This time there was a brief pause. "I hear you and Gorilla had a close call on the golf course. Gorilla says you have steering problems." He chuckled.

I didn't say anything. I kept my eyes on the screen. The silence became more and more uncomfortable. After a minute or two I heard Coach Brogan turn and

118

walk back into our entry hall. I heard my mom's light footsteps descend the steps. "Good-bye, Ron," she called. "Good luck with dinner."

"Bye," I shouted back. The door closed behind them. Even with the television playing loud, I heard the car doors slam and the coach's car engine growl into life. He gave it a few seconds to warm up. Then the sound of the engine got fainter and fainter as he backed down the driveway and headed off down the street. For a moment I thought of Kris and her red Honda CR2 and how she had driven me down to the reservoir. I felt a sharp pang of loneliness.

I watched four hours of television. I watched an old movie, the news, and a "Star Trek" episode I had seen a half dozen times before. A couple of times I got up and paced from room to room. I yanked open the fridge and looked at the meat loaf, all laid out in silver foil with instructions taped on top. There was never any question in my mind that I wouldn't taste a bit of it. I walked into the dining room and saw that Mom had put the roses in our best vase. I hurried out to get away from the sweet smell. I came back to our living room and stood in front of the picture of my father that hung on the side of the mantel. When Coach Brogan had come to dinner and I had taken the picture down, my mom had found it. She had hung it back up and never mentioned it. I took the photograph down again. I turned off the TV and carried the picture of my father up to my room.

I lay in bed with my lamp focused on the picture. Dad looked so young. He must have shaved just before the picture was taken because the skin around his cheeks gleamed smooth. His goofy smile was so similar to my own that it almost felt like I was looking in a mirror rather than at a picture. I wondered what he was thinking about when the picture was taken. His smile radiated both happiness and contentment—his eyes had a peaceful quality, as if he had been searching for something and had finally found it. I kind of sensed that at the moment the photographer snapped the picture, my dad had been thinking about my mom.

Coach Brogan's car pulled up in front of our house at eleven-seventeen. I switched off my lamp and pretended to be fast asleep. I heard their footsteps on the front porch, and then they were inside the house. "Thank you so much," my mom said in a low voice. I sensed that she knew I was awake. "I haven't had such a good time in years."

"I'd like to go out again," I heard Coach Brogan tell her. "Would that be okay with you?"

"I'm already looking forward to it," she told him.

There was a silence. "May I?" I heard him ask in a loud whisper. I didn't hear her answer, but after a second there came the unmistakable sound of a long kiss. I shut my eyes so tight I could see spots against the blackness. Then he left, and she closed and locked the door and climbed the stairs.

She was soon asleep in her room—I could hear her even, level breathing. I tried to sleep, too, but I had no luck at all. I turned on the lamp and studied the picture again, noting the way the uniform showed the muscles on his arms. He had been a strong man. His thick neck pressed all around against the starched collar

120

of his uniform. Despite his obvious strength, he didn't look to me like a fighter.

"How dare you take that again!" My mom woke me up by shaking me. I had fallen asleep with my lamp on and the picture in my arms. She tugged it away. I let it go. "I didn't say anything when you took it the first time, but this has gone too far."

I looked at her. "Have a nice time last night?"

"Very nice," she said. Then, "Ron, I'm not sure what to do, but I will not permit this to continue."

"What?"

"How dare you be rude to Dan last night. Did you think you were hurting me by not eating the dinner I left for you? Why do you keep taking this picture—I don't think you've looked at it more than twice in the past five years."

I lay there looking at her. "Can I shower and get dressed?" I asked.

There was a lot of suppressed anger in her face as she nodded and stood up. "We'll talk at breakfast."

"I don't think I'm hungry."

"I said we'll talk at breakfast," she snapped and walked out.

We had cereal. I had Cheerios, and my mom had Special K. She uses a lot of milk in hers, but I only put in a few trickles. I hate soggy cereal.

"I will not permit it," she said again. "And I think you know what I'm talking about."

"I don't think either of us knows what you're talking about," I told her.

She put her spoon down. "Well, then, I'll spell it

121

out for you. Self-destructive behavior. Rudeness. Laziness. And worst of all, cowardice."

"In what way am I being a coward?"

"If there is something that you don't believe in and that you want to fight, then by all means fight it. But you're not fighting anything. You're just retreating, curling up into yourself further and further."

"I'm keeping up with my schoolwork," I told her. "I'm getting good grades. Isn't there a point where my behavior is my own business?"

"Your behavior was inexcusable last night," she said. "Dan felt hurt and I was shocked. Not eating your dinner was childish. And taking that picture off the wall to try to make me feel guilty was cruel."

"Why would I try to make you feel guilty?" We were talking just below the shouting barrier. Both of our voices swelled till they were almost out of control.

"Because you think in some way I'm being disloyal to your father and to you," she said.

"That's ridiculous," I told her. I stood up. "And I'm getting out of here."

"Why don't you sit down and confront your problems and be a man?" she said.

It was a dangerous moment. I could feel my anger level shooting up the way it does when I think about Igor. "You have no right to say that to me," I told her.

"I have every right. I'm tired of seeing you run away from your feelings about your own father. It's like he's been chasing you for years—a long-dead man wrapped up in all your complicated fears and beliefs and angers—your own personal mummy. I will not stand by and watch you wreck your life because you can't face him."

Her eyes were hard, and my muscles were tensed. I desperately wanted to defuse the situation before it exploded. "Let's drop it," I begged. "You've said enough."

She kept right on going. "I will not tolerate cowardice. Your father faced things head on and solved them. . . ."

"*Yeah?*" I shouted, "*well, maybe he could have taught me something about being a man if he had lived. But he didn't; he wasn't there for me. So to hell with him. And to hell with you too.*" I stormed out of the kitchen and up to my room. I lay on my bed for a while. It had been the biggest fight my mom and I had ever had, and I still felt dizzy.

My mind kept returning to what she had said about my father. I couldn't jog it away. I asked myself if he was really at the root of all my problems. My daddy the mummy; a psychologist would have a great time with that one. I wrapped the pillow around my head, but I still couldn't stop thinking about it—my father and Igor, my personal monsters.

After about half an hour, she knocked at my door. "Ron?"

"Yes?"

"Can I come in?"

"Why?"

"I have something I want to give you." She came in then, looking all upset but also extremely deliberate.

She was holding a bunch of blue papers in her hands. She walked over to the bed. "I want to give you something precious," she said.

I lay there. I didn't know what was coming. My emotions swirled about like a dangerous whirlpool.

"These are letters that your father wrote to me the last week of his life. I probably should have let you read them before, but they're very . . . personal. And you never showed any interest in how your father died. So I kept them. Here . . ." She extended her hand with the letters toward me. There was something special about the way her hands held the pieces of blue paper. It was like she was handing me a rare religious document, an explanation of her whole creed.

"No," I said. "I don't want to read letters to you. I'm sorry we fought, Mom. Let's just go back to the way it was."

"They're not just to me. They're to you, too."

"To me?"

"Take them," she said.

"No. I really don't want to."

"You really do want to," she said. "Find enough courage to get to know your father. You may find that you like him." She placed the letters on the side of the bed and walked out of my room.

THERE WERE SIX LETTERS. The paper was thin and old, and the handwriting was in black pen and neat, the way my own writing has always been neat. They were air letters, with postal directions in French. I unfolded the first one. It was dated March 1, 1970. I read the first two sentences.

Ruth darling,
In the darkness I imagine you are with me, beside me. I undress you, and hold your body next to my own, and make love to you slowly and gently.

I stopped. I couldn't read these love letters. It was too weird. I put them aside and headed off to school. All day at school I thought about them sitting on the edge of my dresser. I thought about the neat handwriting and the fact that my mom said the letters were written to both of us. As soon as I got home I hurried up to my room and read the first one through:

Ruth darling,

In the darkness I imagine you are with me, beside me. I undress you, and hold your body next to my own, and make love to you slowly and gently. I have never needed you more than now. Your warmth. Your goodness. Your brightness. Your love and compassion.

I killed for the first time yesterday. I'm the point man now, which means that when our platoon moves, I lead the way. It's a dangerous job, but it's not something I could refuse. We were moving slowly and quietly through the jungle when an NVA soldier suddenly blundered right into us. I froze. He pointed his gun at me but it didn't go off—it must have jammed. Without thinking I raised my M-16 and shot him in the chest. I was looking right into his eyes when I shot him. He was about my own age. I saw surprise and disbelief—he could not believe that he was about to die. After I shot him he lay on the ground twisting and turning and making horrible sounds.

Ever since then, I've had a premonition of my own death. I hope we'll read this together some day, back in our home in New Jersey, and have a good laugh at how a little combat spooked me. But I can't shake the feeling that just as I took a life, I will soon have my own life taken away. The

126

feeling grows and grows. I wish I could talk to you. I am lying awake, imagining the sound of your voice.

Got to go now. We're moving out. If anything should happen to me, one of my buddies will bring you these letters. I think of you with every step I take in this steamy jungle. I love you.

I folded the letter very carefully. I didn't want to read any further, but I couldn't stop myself from taking the next letter off the stack and opening it up.

Ruth darling,

It's been hell ever since I arrived in Vietnam, but this morning was more hell and deeper hell than I ever experienced before. I wish this mission was over. The feeling that I am going to die keeps growing stronger.

I mentioned it to Sergeant Martinson and he laughed and told me he's felt the same way a hundred times. I pray that he is right.

This morning our platoon entered a small village near Bu Dop. We had reports that an NVA sniper might be hiding in the village. It seemed like any other village, and at first there was no trouble. We rounded up the villagers and while Sergeant Martinson and Nguyen, our interpreter, questioned them, we searched the village from hut to hut. We found only stores of rice, skinny dogs, and water buffalo. We were just searching the last few huts when a machine gun opened up on us from one side, and a mortar began pitching death at us from some distant trees. The villagers were just as surprised as we were; we all scrambled to take cover.

A bullet went through my ammo can, and other bullets were hitting metal or kicking up dust all around me. The explosions of the mortar's shells thudded closer and closer. My best friend, Pfc Jack Osborne, went down right next to me. I've written to you about him before. He came here from Grundy Center, Iowa, where he raised hogs and owned a small farm. He was married and had two little girls. During all these months of hell I've never heard him complain even once. He's carried a Bible with him on every mission, and sometimes he reads passages from it in a big, open voice that made you think of Iowa cornfields. Anyway, I managed to drag him behind a rock and then I slipped on top of him, covering him with my body. But it was too late—he was dead.

For twenty minutes or so it was like a hailstorm of death. I squeezed off a few rounds of the machine gun, but for the most part I just kept pressed as close as I could to the rock. Suddenly the enemy mortar and machine-gun fire stopped. I don't know why. Sergeant Martinson had called in for an air strike, and maybe the guys who had ambushed us had enough experience to know when to leave.

In addition to Osborne, I lost two other friends. Phillips and Mellen both died during the ambush. I don't know why I was allowed to live when better men were taken, but there's no reason or logic to this war. I guess I survived because I found a rock to hide behind. It's that simple.

Two copters came and removed our dead and wounded, but the rest of us are continuing through the jungle. We're supposed to link up with some forces in Bu Dop. The jungle is dank and my skin is alive with leeches and bugs. We've been living off C rations. As we march, my mind keeps wandering back to our hometown on a Sunday morning. I know it's crazy, but I keep thinking of the two of us as parents with four or five or six kids sitting around a big wooden table. A couple of waffle irons send out clouds of sweet smells. Our kids look happy and hungry. We have pure Vermont maple syrup and butter and brown sugar. Ron, our oldest son, is digging into the first waffle with hungry haste. He's six, or maybe seven. He looks like you and smiles like me, and the combination is winning.

I gotta go now. I'll write again soon. I miss you so much I can barely stand it.

I folded that letter up and put it on top of the first one. My mom had never cooked waffles during my entire childhood. The third letter was very short. I found myself holding my breath as I read it.

Ruth darling,

Just a note as we stop for lunch. We marched all day, and I spent the time thinking about our senior prom. The theme song, "The Long and

Winding Road," kept playing in my head. I remember the yellow dress you wore, and the trouble I had pinning the corsage on it. You were so beautiful that night. Do you remember the first time we slow danced? Neither of us really knew what steps to take, but it didn't matter at all. I remember how my hands slid down to your hips and around your back, and I felt dizzy and bursting with energy at the same time. I wondered for the first time if I could be in love.

Gotta go.

I folded it up. There's a picture from that senior prom in one of the photo albums downstairs. My mom looks very pretty and very young and is wearing a long yellow dress. My dad is wearing a jacket and tie and has his arm around my mom's waist. I could imagine him walking through the jungles of Vietnam thinking about that night and using the memory to keep himself going.

Ruth darling,

I couldn't sleep last night. The feeling that I am going to die hovered around my head like an insect, stinging me awake whenever I began to drift off. Oddly, I was never tired and lay there thinking about you and our baby and the life I left behind. It was one of the longest nights of my life.

When dawn came I took out the picture of Ron that you sent—the one where he's lying in his crib—and I saw it as if for the very first time.

130

Why did I ever think he looks like you? This morning as I looked at the picture I saw myself in our baby's face. I saw my eyes in his eyes, my hair in his hair, my chin and cheeks in the lines of his face, and even my big dopey grin in his baby's smile. Seeing myself in my son was a great comfort to me and for a little while the feeling of impending death that had been keeping me awake all night went away, and I grabbed an hour's nap.

There were two more letters. The next one was in bad condition and I had to struggle to make out some of the words. The letter had been creased and folded over many times, and the black ink was so faint in spots that I had to figure words out by context and by piecing together the readable letters.

Ruth darling,

We spent the day slogging through an endless marsh. The leeches are awful, and I've seen snakes and all sorts of other nasty things. Just before noon the last man in our column, Tibbs, stepped on a land mine. It was the kind we call a Bouncing Betty, because when you step on it it hops up into the air and then explodes. Thank God we were spaced out pretty well and Tibbs was trailing at a wide distance. He was killed instantly, but the next guy forward received only minor wounds.

The Vietnamese villagers have the most innocent faces. As we march through villages they gather to stare at us. They have thin, curious faces and the children have quick, playful eyes. All the eyes seem to silently ask us the same question: What are a bunch of young American men doing here?

One of the things that haunts me most is that I probably could have avoided the draft. A lot of my friends found ways to keep out of the war. When I was drafted, I never even thought about not coming. I just thought it was my duty and that somehow I would get through. Such an important decision made so quickly, easily, and blindly! If I don't come back, I hope you won't begin to hate me for the way I destroyed two, no three, lives. I think a lot about what life will be like for you and Ron without me.

Remember that Hemingway story, "The Snows of Kilimanjaro" that Mr. Otis made us read in senior English? In the story, as the main character lies dying, he sees death coming close to him and he imagines it to be two bicycle policemen. I remember when I read it I thought it was a beautiful image, and that Hemingway had to have some special knowledge because it had the ring of truth. Well, approaching death doesn't feel that way to me at all. It's not an image or a picture or a sound or a smell or anything familiar. It's more like a shadow than anything else. Not a shadow cast by the sun, but a shadow that stays around me even at night when I'm lying in my cot.

Ruth, if something should happen to me, I want you to make a new life. You're young and pretty and wonderful and I'm sure there will be lots of guys. And Ron will need a father. I'm serious now. I'm saying this even though it hurts worse than anything else I could possibly say to you. I look into the future and see you with another man and I hate him for being close to you. I wish I could shoot him with this gun that is always next to me. I wish I could kill him with my bare hands. But, at the same time, I want you to have him. I know it will be for the best. I will always be Ron's true father no matter who raises him or what he turns out like. And the love we had between us will always be there, even if I am not.

I tucked it away and picked up the last letter. It was dated March 6. It was the longest letter of the bunch. The writing was firm and sure—there were no crossed-out words or false beginnings or rephrased endings. Rather, it was as if my father had been writing from a special private reserve of great sense and clarity.

Ruth darling,
    I woke up today and I knew. Don't ask me how but I finally knew for sure. I don't feel afraid so much as sad. I wish I could see you one more time. I wish I could touch your lips and your eyelids and brush back your hair and run a long kiss down your neck. I wish I could hold my son in my arms once. But I know none of these things will happen, so I am going to try to face death like a man.
    The thoughts that have run through my head in the last few days! This morning when I woke

up I lay still for a while and my mind drifted forward over the years yet to be. I keep a picture of you and a picture of Ron in my front chest pocket, over my heart. You both look so young.

What will he look like at ten? At fifteen? What will he look like when he pulls back his arm to throw a football for the first time? When he goes out on his first date? When he graduates from college? Will he know me at all? Will he love me? Hate me? Understand me?

I'm going to give these letters to a good friend of mine to bring to you. Show them to Ron when he is old enough to understand them. This morning as I lay there, I lived an entire imaginary life with my son. I took him to a Yankee game and bought him hot dogs with mustard, and we moved down to the first row and shouted ourselves hoarse. And I took him fishing for bass and showed him how to bait the hook and cast it out far to the lily pads, and then we lay back on the shore and talked about sports and girls. And I was there when he graduated from high school, one of the crowd of fathers snapping pictures and beaming with pride.

So I speak directly to you, Ron, through the years if this letter ever gets to you and you ever read it. I love you the way a father loves a good son, even if I can't be there to help you through difficult years. I don't have any great advice to give you, but I want you to know that on the last day of my life I spent a long time thinking about you and trying to be with you. The more I have read about the men I most admire in all of history—men like Christ, Lincoln, and Gandhi—the more I have become convinced that what made them great was a softness underneath their commitment to a creed or cause. A gentleness. They all seemed to understand the weakness and frailty of being human, and to be able to understand and forgive at the deepest levels. It is the one quality I hope and pray you develop, my son: the strength to love, understand, and forgive.

Ruth, time feels like it is growing short. There are too many things for me to write to you, too many even for me to say. I kiss you good-bye with as much love and regret as any soldier ever felt since the world began. God bless you and keep you. God turn your sadness into joy, and make your mourning pass. We are about to begin our march. It is a bright day and the sky above the jungle is clear through the tangle of trees and vines. I am ready for what lies ahead.

I read that last letter over two or three times, and then I went back and read the whole bunch over and over again. Each time I read one, I seemed to focus on a different line or phrase and find new meanings and emotions in the hastily written lines.

Mom called me down to dinner at six-thirty.

"Can I keep those letters?" I asked her.

She shook her head. "I want them back," she said. "You can have them for a few more days, but they belong to me." She didn't ask me if I had finished reading them or what I had thought of them. I guess she could tell by looking at my face.

"Mom, who brought them to you?"

"A friend of your father's. Sam Parker. He's . . . disabled. His brother drove him all the way here from Washington, D.C., so that he could deliver them to me by hand. It was nice of him. We still exchange Christmas cards." She lifted a pot of beef stew off the burner. "Now sit down and let's eat."

"I'm not hungry," I said. "I gotta go for a walk."

If I had said this on any normal night, my mother would have insisted that I sit and eat the meal she had cooked. She's a pretty stern disciplinarian, and she expects me to follow her rules. On this night she just looked at me and nodded. "If you want some later, all you have to do is reheat it," she said.

I walked out alone down Sylvan Avenue. It was a cold, clear night. I headed down to Lakeview Road and took the narrow path around the lake. The wind whistled through the leafless limbs with a long, shrill sound. Gusts kicked up snow on the flat surface of the frozen lake.

I thought about my father as he must have been in the last few days of his life. He had been only a few years older than I was now. He must have been frightened, but a calmness ran through the last letter, as if he had accepted his fate. The paragraph he addressed to me was strange—it was as if he was reaching out across the years to try to touch me even as death closed in around him. There, on the shores of the frozen lake, I tried to throw my mind back two decades

136

to a steamy Vietnam jungle and touch him. For years I
had brooded about how my father wasn't there for me
at crucial moments in my life. Now, on this walk, I
relived those moments and tried to imagine that he was
indeed with me, standing by my side. He was in the
stands at wrestling matches. He gave me advice about
Kris. He helped me train to face Igor. We went bass
fishing together. He told me war stories about his days
in Vietnam and about how he had once been so
spooked he thought he was going to die.

I walked and I thought and I went back over those
letters in my mind, right up until the final line of the
last letter. That day he had died. He had fallen beneath the same bright sky he had described in his last
few lines. As I turned back toward our house, I suddenly knew what I had to do.

My mom was still awake when I got home. "Want
some stew?"

I nodded, and she heated me up a serving. "Have a
nice walk?"

"Mom," I told her, "I want to take a few days off
from school. I'd like to go on a trip."

She looked at me. "Where?"

"To Washington, D.C. I'd like to see Sam Parker."

I thought for sure she would refuse, or at least
argue, but she accepted my plan as if she knew I had
to do it. "I'll give you some money for tickets and
a hotel room," she said. "I want you to be careful.
Washington is dangerous."

"I'm going to stay with Sam," I told her.

She gave me another quizzical glance, as if to ask
how I knew, when I had never even talked to Sam

137

Parker. But she didn't argue. "Take the money anyway," she said. "I'd feel better knowing you had it."

She sat down across from me as I ate the stew. "I'll come back on Sunday afternoon so I can go to school on Monday," I told her.

She smiled. "For years I've made you go to school every single day. Even when you pretended to be sick. This time, stay away as long as you need to."

"Thanks," I told her.

"You're welcome," she said. "I just hope you find what you're looking for."

I HAD NEVER BEEN to Washington, D.C., before. My mom had given me the address on Sam's last Christmas card, and I managed to find his apartment building without trouble. It wasn't in a particularly good neighborhood. The policeman on the Metro platform who gave me directions told me to be careful, and I tried to follow his advice. I kept on the well-lit side of the street, and I walked fast and purposefully. I felt a few people look at me, but I hurried by them and no one said anything.

Sam lived in a very old but reasonably clean building. I took the stairs rather than the elevator and walked up three flights to apartment 3F. I rang the bell. Nothing happened. I rang it again. Still nothing. I was just getting ready to leave when the door opened very fast and a black man in a wheelchair pointed a gun at my head.

I froze. I guess I must have looked surprised, but I think he looked even more surprised than I did. He kept staring at my face, and his large eyes looked like they would swell out and pop with disbelief. "I thought I'd lost all the ghosts," he whispered to himself. His hand, holding the gun, was absolutely steady.

Finally I found my voice. "I'm Ron Woods. I'm looking for Sam Parker. He . . . was a friend of my father."

"And your father was Jim Woods?" he asked in a deep, low voice. "Jim Woods from Jersey?"

"That's right."

He lowered his gun. He had the most complicated face I had ever seen in my life. The combination of inner strength and inner weakness made the large eyes and flat nose and proud chin a puzzle to try to figure out. He had a mustache that drooped around the corners of his mouth. His arms, which rested on the wheels of his wheelchair, were enormous. "Come in," he said. "And close the door behind you."

I entered his apartment and closed the door. I followed him down a narrow hallway to the living room. His apartment was very clean and filled with unusual objects. A red Oriental lantern cover enabled the overhead light to cast scarlet patterns on the white walls. He motioned me to sit down in the one armchair. He wheeled his wheelchair close to me and spent a minute or two examining my face.

"You know how much you look like him?" he asked.

I shook my head.

"I thought I was seeing a ghost," he said. "For years after I came back, I saw ghosts all the time, but I've managed to lose them one by one. When I saw you, I thought your father was standing at my door."

"Were you good friends?" I asked him.

"We were friends," he nodded. "Don't get me wrong—there were people I was closer to. But your daddy was a good man. I always liked him."

The photographs on the walls showed exotic Asian scenes. A faint smell of incense sweetened the air in the room. Oriental weapons hung on racks. There were swords and knives and nunchooks and what looked like tridents, and other things I couldn't identify. Sam Parker smiled at my examination of his apartment. "Can I get you a beer?" he asked.

"I don't drink."

"Neither did your father," he recalled. "It was one of the things I didn't like about him. I don't trust a man who doesn't drink now and then. You sure?"

I nodded. He rolled himself into the kitchen and came back with a can of beer and a can of Coke. He handed me the Coke and opened the beer, and then he said, "All right, Ron, now that you're here, what can I do for you?"

He waited. I didn't know what to say. There were no clocks in the room, and time seemed to slip by even more slowly than usual. "I don't really know much about my father," I finally told him.

"Your mother doesn't talk about him?" he wanted to know. I shook my head. "Fine woman, your mother. As good as he always said she was. She's still healthy

141

and happy?" I nodded. "Good. I liked her. Now what do you want me to do?"

"Tell me anything you can remember," I asked him. "I just read the letters you brought home so I know a little bit about what it was like . . . but I'd like to hear more. I'd like to hear how my father died."

Sam looked at me long and hard. "You read a few letters and you think you know what it was like? You don't know nothing. You could read every book on Vietnam and see every movie and still know nothing. And I can't tell you what it was like either. It was something you had to live through. Or die in."

He was silent a long time, lost in his memories. I waited. Gradually his eyes refocused on me, and he smiled. "You are so much like him. The same big dumb smile. The same quiet good manners."

"What was he like? How did he spend his time?"

Sam closed his eyes and tilted his head back. "He was a very strong and gentle guy. Everyone kind of liked him. He read more than anyone in our platoon. Early in the morning when we were in camp I would always find him with a book in his hands. All different books, too. I remember he was reading about religious leaders and great generals and statesmen—like he was looking for a hero. Someone to follow.

"Was good at sports. Not great but good. He was a little guy like yourself, but really put together. In football games he'd tackle anyone. In boxing he'd step in with much heavier guys. Never whored, never drank, never smoked, and I don't think he prayed much either. Just a tough, self-sufficient guy trying to survive."

"Did he talk about my mom a lot?"

142

Sam finished his beer and shot it across the room so that it fell into a wastebasket about twenty feet away. "Are you kidding? That's all he talked about. Your mom and you. He used to carry around a picture of you lying in your crib and show it off to anyone who would look."

"And do you know how he felt about the war? About fighting in Vietnam?"

Sam smiled at me, and there was a laugh of derision hidden just below the surface of that smile. "Ron, we were trying to survive, okay? Don't look too deep." He yawned. "I go to sleep pretty early. You want to stay here tonight? I got a bedroll you can sleep in."

I took the bedroll out of the closet and spread it out on the floor. Sam brought a blanket and a clean pillow. "You get some sleep," he said. "I'm glad you came. It took you a long time, but your father was a good man and I'm glad you care."

I fell asleep almost immediately and had very strange dreams. I dreamed that I was in the jungle myself, hunting for Igor. Kris was there, too, and Coach Brogan and Gorilla. I could never catch up with Igor, but I could hear him laughing as he floated through the jungle just out of sight.

I dreamed that Sam Parker and I were playing football and that I was afraid to tackle a certain big player. Sam took one of his swords down from the rack and put the point at my throat and told me to make the tackle or die.

I woke up early the next morning, but Sam was already up and dressed. When I came out of the shower, he had a small but good breakfast laid out on the table. There was coffee, biscuits, jam, juice, and a little fruit. "Sleep well?" he asked.

"Strange dreams," I told him.

He nodded. "You came all this way by yourself to ask me a few questions about your father; I figure something big must be bothering you."

I nodded but didn't explain, and he didn't push me. We ate in silence for a while. "You can stay as long as you want," he said. "I can't feed you lunch and dinner, but you can sleep here."

I ended up staying for two days. During that time I found out tiny bits and pieces of information about my father. It was like I was gathering pieces of a puzzle, and I hoped that when I had them all together I would be able to see his image clearly. I found out that Dad had cut his own hair and that he had a terrible singing voice but loved to whistle and that he was known for having a big appetite. I learned that he was a devoted Yankee fan who followed all the scores and that he occasionally talked about wanting to go to college when his tour was done.

On Sunday morning I told Sam I was ready to leave.

"I don't know if I've helped you any," he said.

"You have." Then I asked him, "Could you tell me how my father died?"

We were sitting in the kitchen drinking strong black coffee. Sunlight streamed in through a small kitchen window. To tell the truth, I like the smell of coffee much more than I like the taste. This coffee had a thick, strong smell. Sam put his cup down.

144

"You really wanna hear about it?"

"Yes," I said. "Please."

"He wasn't a hero or anything, and I'm not gonna lie to you."

"I just want to know."

Sam nodded. He brought his two large fists together and rubbed his knuckles into his forehead. He had a lot of strange gestures like that. During the time that I had stayed with him he hadn't talked about himself at all. I didn't know how he had become paralyzed or if he had a job or even if he was happy with his life. Sometimes he seemed content and at peace, and other times he seemed so frustrated and angry he frightened me. I hadn't told him much about myself. We had gotten to know each other through my questions and his memories of my father.

Now, for the first time, he revealed something of himself. "I believe that death is the final test of manhood," he said. "You can tell everything about a man by the way he faces death. In 'Nam I saw men cry and crawl, and I saw others die silently or curse death with their last breaths. I saw that rarest of all things—a man sacrificing his life for his friends. And I saw cowards endanger the whole platoon through their fear."

He leaned closer to me. I put down my coffee cup and listened closely. "Now your father's death," he said, "was unusual. I think it was a good death, but it had its own special quality." He rapped his knuckles on the table, as if summoning up a specter from the past. He was silent for a time, and then he nodded and smiled a thin, hard smile.

"I remember it was March 6," he said. "I remem-

145

ber the dates. Every year I go down to the memorial on certain days and lay some flowers down for a dead buddy. On March 6 I go down for your daddy."

His face slowly took on a faraway look. His eyes became quick—they jumped from me around the room and back to me again. "That morning your daddy gave me the letters. I didn't want to take them. 'You'll mail those yourself,' I told him. He shook his head. He had been talking about dying for days, and the way he shook his head gave me the creeps. 'Then, if something happens to you, I'll take them and deliver them. I don't need them now.' Again he shook his head and tried to hand them to me. So I took them. Six of them. And he smiled and thanked me.

"That was a nightmare mission, and we had reached the worst day of the nightmare. We were all sick from the bugs and leeches and constant fear. It wears you down. We were going through heavy jungle, and it was a hard choice whether you wanted to look down for land mines or up in the trees for snipers. There had been a lot of fighting in the area—not just us but other units, too. Heavy fighting.

"About noon we passed through a small village, and a couple of the boys were a little rough with some of the villagers." A shadow passed across Sam's face. "You gotta remember this was a war. Anyway, it was ugly. We started away from the village and suddenly a girl—maybe fifteen years old—ran from a path onto the road and headed straight for your father. She was dressed in black pajamas.

"I didn't see her at first, but your father saw her and shouted for her to stop. He shouted it in English

146

and then in Vietnamese. But the girl kept on running. She had a weird smile on her face, and she yelled back at him in singsong Vietnamese. He yelled again. She got closer. He raised his M-16 and pointed it at her, but he never shot. Instead, he lowered it. I guess he couldn't shoot a young girl like that who didn't seem to understand his command to stop."

Sam halted his story momentarily. "Your daddy had killed an NVA soldier a few days before, and it had been bothering him. I don't think he had gotten any sleep since, and that's what started him talking about how he was going to die. Maybe that's why he lowered his gun. I don't know. When I saw what he was doing, I raised mine to shoot her, but it was too late. She ran right up to him as if she was going to embrace him. I think she might have even thrown her arms around him, or at least that's the illusion I had at the time. Then she set off her grenade. When the smoke cleared, we tried to find as many of the pieces as we could, but they were scattered pretty well and it was hard to tell what was from the girl and what was from your daddy. Anyway, that's how he died. I don't know for sure, but I think he knew she had the grenade when he lowered his gun. Not a bad death."

I sat there for a long time. He didn't say anything. He poured himself another cup of coffee and sipped it slowly, rolling the hot black coffee around in the back of his mouth. I think I could have sat there for hours and he wouldn't have said a word to disturb me. He seemed to have a deep understanding of privacy and silence.

"I should go," I finally told him.

147

"You seen Washington at all?" he asked me.

"No, I came straight here. And during the days I've been walking around this neighborhood in a kind of daze, thinking."

"Why don't you take a look at the city on your way home? Stop at the War Memorial."

"What's that?"

He looked at me fast and shook his head. "The Vietnam War Memorial. You found your way here—find your way there. And listen, say hello to your mother for me. Tell her Sam wishes her well."

"I'll tell her," I promised. I got my stuff together, and he wheeled himself to the door to see me out. "Thanks," I said.

We shook hands. He had an iron grip. "You make your mom proud of you," he said. "Whatever's eating at you, don't let it swallow you up. Hear?" The heavy door swung shut behind me.

I DIDN'T HEAD DIRECTLY for the Vietnam War Memorial. I got off the Metro at Capitol Hill and spent about an hour looking at the buildings I had read so much about. The Capitol building was huge and impressive, and I could hear the speeches of Daniel Webster ringing in my ears as I looked at the vast structure.

The Supreme Court building was smaller, but to me even more impressive. Many of the cases and laws that I had read about for years in my room back home had been fought out in this building. It was still early on a Sunday morning, and all the buildings were closed, so I stood on the pavement looking up the steep slope of white steps and tried to imagine the Supreme Court justices presiding. Perhaps one day the question of mandatory drug testing of high school athletes would be fought out here once and for all. For the first time in a while, I thought back to the drug test and the position I had taken, and I felt good about having stood up for my beliefs. There was something about being on Capitol Hill, in front of the Supreme Court, that inspired me.

I walked around for a while more and looked at the House and Senate office buildings, where the actual day-to-day work of the Congress is done. And I passed the Library of Congress, where the new books and art and ideas of the entire nation are patented and catalogued and stored. And I got a strong feeling that I belonged in this place and that I should try to come back here some day as a page or a summer intern or even for a career. Capitol Hill was just electric for me. The sense of tradition and power and history in the making was tremendous.

I walked down the back steps of the Capitol building and headed along the grassy Mall toward the Washington Monument. The white marble of the monument gleamed in the morning sun. Around me on parts of the Mall's grass a couple of touch-football games were starting up. It was a cold, clear day. Everywhere I looked I seemed to see a building I had read about. I looked to my left and saw the Smithsonian Institute.

A young couple passed by on my right, holding hands and laughing happily. The girl had long blonde hair, and her flirtatious smile reminded me forcefully of Kris. She gave her boyfriend a playful nip on the neck, and he swung her around and hugged her. I watched them together, and I regretted not having returned Kris's phone calls for the past few weeks. I had been so wrapped up in my own problems I hadn't thought about what she must have been feeling. Now that I was coming to the end of my lonely quest, I missed her.

I paused for a little while by the Washington Monument. It's such a simple structure. I fixed it in my memory as best I could and then set off for the Lincoln Memorial. It was a beautiful walk. The surface of the Reflecting Pool was absolutely still. The statue of Lincoln facing out of the memorial building grew closer and closer, until I could finally see his famous face. Lincoln was one of my heroes, and I knew from the letters that he had been one of my father's heroes, too. The magnificent statue seemed to catch the graceful humanity of the man, just as the speeches inscribed on the walls of the memorial repeated his eloquent patriotism.

I turned right from the Lincoln Memorial, and I soon reached my destination. The Vietnam War Memorial was very different from the other monuments I had seen that morning. First I looked at the bronze statue of three soldiers—one black, one white, and one Hispanic—frozen in midmarch with their weapons in their hands. The statue does not glorify the soldiers. Their faces show both fear and determination, commitment and confusion. But there is something about the closeness and physical contact between the soldiers that reminded me of the way my dad wrote about his friends in the unit and the way Sam Parker had spoken about

151

my father. I got a sense of the bonds of friendship and respect that the men who had gone through the ordeal had forged with one another.

Then I walked over to the wedge of black granite that seems to sink into the ground. The granite is highly polished, and the black color lends the monument a slightly somber, decorous majesty. The Washington Monument and the Lincoln Memorial are high, soaring structures proclaiming greatness. I liked the way this simple black wedge cut through the green grass to make its point in a restrained, understated way.

Capitol Hill had been pretty empty, and the Mall had been deserted in spots, but there were people standing and looking all along the Vietnam War Memorial. At the foot of many of the black granite panels visitors had placed bunches of flowers or small American flags.

I walked down the wedge, following the deaths in chronological order from panel to panel. I reached the area where the names were from March of 1970 and stood there scanning the columns for my own last name. It felt weird to be looking for my own name on a memorial so close to the Lincoln and Washington monuments. And then I saw it. JAMES WOODS. Just that. Carved into the black granite at about shoulder height.

My mom had never come to Washington, so as far as I knew, I was the first member of Dad's family to see his name up there. The morning was wintry and windless, cold and still. I very slowly reached out my right index finger and touched the roof of the J in JAMES. My finger started to shake, but I kept going

152

as I traced out his name letter by letter. And when I got to his last name—my own last name—the floodgates suddenly burst, and I felt tears streaming down my face as my whole body shivered. My finger continued. W–O–O–D–S, and if it is at all possible to touch the past, I did it in those moments. I touched a man almost my own age, a gentle, strong man who cut his own hair and followed the Yankees' box scores and liked to whistle. The polished granite was cool beneath my finger, and when I was done I just leaned against it and let the tears continue to fall.

"Excuse me, are you okay?" An old woman stood next to me, her eyes warm with concern. I looked at her through a mist of tears and emotion. She smiled. "I just wanted to make sure you were all right."

I pushed myself away from the panel. "Thanks," I said, wiping my face on my sleeve. My voice came out a tiny bit hoarse. "It's been a little tough but . . . I'm all right." I took a deep breath of the cold morning air. "I feel fine now."

I DIDN'T GET BACK HOME till after dinner time. A bus dropped me off on the corner of Sylvan Avenue, and I walked up to my house through the lengthening shadows. I guess my mom and Coach Brogan were kissing on the couch because as I came through the door I heard them hurriedly moving apart, and when I walked into the living room, they both looked very embarrassed. "Hi," I told them. "Just me, back from my travels."

"Did you have a good trip?" my mother asked, and I understood the deeper question within her question.

"Yes," I nodded. "Sam sends his regards. This morning I stopped off at the Vietnam War Memorial and found Dad's name. You should see it sometime."

My mom looked just a tiny bit uncomfortable, and I realized I should try not to talk about my dad while

Mom was sitting on the couch next to Coach Brogan. "Anyway," I said, "it's nice to be home." I sniffed the air. "There's nothing like home cooking."

"So you haven't eaten yet?" my mother asked. A minute later she was in the kitchen getting together a plate of leftovers for me. I guess since I had been away a few days, she sort of missed fussing over me. "You get pretty good service here, Ron," Coach Brogan said with a laugh. "Dinner served whenever you want it."

Despite his smiles and laughs, I could feel a bit of tension between me and Coach Brogan. Part of the awkwardness was left over from when I had been rude to him the night he took my mom out to dinner, and I think the rest came from the fact that he just didn't know how to relate to me now that he was becoming close to my mother. I decided to be direct. "I'm sorry for being rude to you the other night," I told him. "I've been going through some hard times."

He put his hand up. "Don't say another word. It's forgotten."

"No," I said, "listen, I owe you an apology and I want to give you one. The truth is it's nice to have you coming over to our house. Nice for my mom and nice for me."

He didn't say anything, but he reached out a huge hand and I took it. His grip was warm and firm.

"Listen," I said, "I know the team is doing badly, and I was wondering if I could come to the practices to watch and maybe help some of the younger wrestlers. I know I'm not allowed to practice myself, but maybe I could be a little help to some of the other guys."

155

"You could be a big help," Coach Brogan admitted, "if you could live through a little hostility. I think some of the guys on the team blame you for our poor season. Most of them have lost the winning attitude. The reason I made you captain is that you kind of radiate that attitude. We could use you a lot."

My mom came in then, carrying a big plate of food for me and some dessert for herself and Coach Brogan. We sat around eating and talking for two or three hours, and it felt very nice and natural to have a third person to joke around with. Once Coach Brogan began laughing, he relaxed and was a lot of fun.

Coach Brogan left at about ten, and his last words as he headed out the door were, "Thanks for the dinner, Ruth. Ron, I'll see you tomorrow."

Then he was gone and I was alone in the house with my mother. "So you had a good trip?" she asked again.

"Sam's a nice guy," I told her. "He told me a lot about Dad."

"And you found what you were looking for?"

I was silent as I thought about it. I really wasn't sure what I had been looking for and what I had found.

"Well, anyway, you seem a lot more at peace," Mom said. Then she walked to the wall and took down the picture of my father in his military uniform, which had already caused so much trouble between us. Her fingers didn't shake at all as she took it down. She carried it over to the couch and sat down next to me. "Would you like to hang this up in your room?"

"You won't miss it down here?"

She looked like she didn't know exactly how she felt or how to phrase her thoughts. "Dan always looks at it when he comes into this room," she finally said. "I always see him stealing glances at it."

"You like him a lot?" I asked.

"Yes," she admitted, "I like him. I feel like I have something to look forward to every day, instead of looking backward."

"I'll take it up to my room," I told her. "It will look good on the wall above my bed."

"Good night," she said, and then she leaned over and kissed me on my forehead. It was a thing she used to do every night when I was young, but she hadn't done it in years.

"Good night, Mom," I said back. "And thanks for putting up with such a crazy son."

"You're not as crazy as you think," she said. "Now go to bed. You've got to get up tomorrow morning for school." She tried to sound a little severe, but we both knew it wasn't working.

"WE'VE GOT A LITTLE LESS than half a season to go," Coach Brogan told the team the next day. "I want to start winning. Ron is going to help me out during practices. I want the underclassmen especially to work with him. I'm going to concentrate on the varsity. We can still turn this season around if everyone gets serious, works hard, and thinks about winning."

It felt good to be back in The Furnace. The door was soon closed and the pipes were dripping, and when wrestling practice started, the temperature seemed to zoom up so quickly you could feel it rise.

Gorilla led the team through warm-up exercises. He grunted out the sets in rapid-fire bursts of energy. I stood in a corner and watched the sit-ups and push-ups and leg raisers and back bridges. I felt like I should be the one out there leading, but it was good to smell the old smells and hear the grunts and groans and watch the familiar routine of repetitions.

Coach Brogan pushed them hard. They did the wall-to-wall four times in a row, and by the last one a lot of the guys were too tired to even attempt to cross the room. Gorilla made it across all four times. He was undefeated so far this year, and he seemed to be wrestling with a good combination of experience and high intensity.

They did the spinning drill until an underclassman had to run to the bathroom and throw up. Two guys do the spinning drill together. One guy gets down on all fours and keeps his head down. The second guy plants his weight on the first guy's back, extends his arms, and spreads his legs to either side so his toes touch the mat. When Coach Brogan yells "Spin," the guy on top uses his feet to whirl around and around on his teammate's back until the coach yells "Stop." If you're not in great shape, you soon get tired and dizzy and have trouble spinning at a steady speed and rhythm.

They worked on technique for a while, and I helped a few freshmen and sophomores who were having trouble with the basics. One tall freshman was having a lot of trouble with posture. The ability to control your body and to carry it in the best possible way is the first step in learning to wrestle. This freshman was trying for a square stance, but he was doing a lot of things wrong and looked out of balance. First I told him to keep his elbows tucked in close to his body and his hands down below his belt level. He had been watching his opponent's face, and I explained to him

159

that he should focus his eyes on his opponent's hips because that was where the first trace of a decision to move would show. Then I worked with him on getting his back straight, so that even though he was in a semisquatting position with his knees bent, his chest was on a plane with his knees.

At first I was kind of hesitant about giving advice, but the guys on the team seemed to welcome suggestions, so I ended up even helping some of the varsity wrestlers. The only guy who didn't like it when I tried to give him advice was Carl Stoner. He had been wrestling all year in my slot at 144 pounds, and he had a mediocre record so far. He looked like he was in great shape, but his eyes were red and baggy, and his disposition was even more sour than I remembered it.

I wasn't going to help him, but I watched him try a difficult pinning combination called the guillotine. He practiced it over and over again, and he kept making the same mistake. He started it off all right by getting a grapevine hold on his opponent's left leg and clamping on an armlock. He then correctly pulled his opponent's arm behind his neck and leaned back and away from him, forcing his opponent onto his back. He locked his legs and applied pressure with his left arm, but he didn't know what to do with his right arm. He tried it in a couple of different spots.

Finally I walked over and said, "Carl, excuse me, but it works best if you use your right arm to hold him securely around the waist and tuck your fingers around his side."

I guess maybe Carl was sensitive about taking advice from me because he was wrestling in my weight class on the varsity. He had taken my slot without beating me. Or maybe he was still mad about the fight we had had. Anyway, his red-rimmed eyes narrowed as he said, "I didn't ask you for help."

"I just thought I could give you a hand. I'm trying to help the team," I said, backing away.

He didn't say anything else, but the hatred that flashed from his eyes was so intense it was almost feverish.

After practice I talked with Coach Brogan for a little while about what I had seen and who needed work. By the time I was ready to head home, most of the guys had showered and left. I started jogging, and after about two blocks I caught up to Stinker and Gorilla. Gorilla looked glad to see me. "It was great that you came today," he said. "I try to help the young guys, but it's hard when I'm wrestling too."

Stinker didn't say anything or even look at me. We hadn't talked since the day he had told me off at the fishing creek. He walked along next to Gorilla, keeping his eyes fixed on the pavement.

"Hey, Stinker," I said.

He didn't look up. "Yeah?"

"How ya doin'?"

"I'm doin' just fine."

"You must be washing your sweats more often than last year. I could barely smell you today."

He looked up at me to see what was going on.

"If you keep that up, we're gonna have to start calling you Rosebud," I told him.

"I gotta stop in here for a second," Gorilla said as we passed Stan's Hardware Store. "Wait for me."

161

Being his usual tactful self, I think, Gorilla was just getting out of the way for a few minutes.

"Whaddya want?" Stinker asked.

"Remember at the fishing creek I said that I didn't know if I wanted to be friends with you or not? Well, I know the answer now. I do."

Stinker didn't say anything. His pinched face was still frozen in serious thought.

"I'm sorry about this wrestling season. I just couldn't take that drug retest. But . . . I mean we've been friends for years and years. Most of our lives. Fishing down at the creek. Wrestling tournaments. Scoping girls out at the mall. Those tackle football games on your front lawn when Gorilla and I used to mash you like a sack of potatoes . . ."

Stinker opened his mouth, and I waited. "You were always a pussy at tackle football," he said.

"I was always afraid I would hurt you."

"You don't know anything about fishing either," he said.

"C'mon, I'm the one who always catches the big ones."

"When we went to the mall, you always spotted the ugliest girls in the whole state," he said.

"Isn't that a subjective opinion?" I asked him.

"And when it comes to football, you were always afraid to try diving tackles. Admit it."

"Only a moron wouldn't be afraid to try to dive tackle Gorilla," I told him.

"Just because Gorilla is a half-ton pile of lard doesn't mean he won't go down if you hit him right," he said.

At that moment Gorilla came out of the hardware store. "Nice to see you guys talking again," he said.

"Yeah, we were just talking about you," I told him. "Stinker said you were a half-ton pile of lard."

Gorilla looked at Stinker. "Coming from a yellow-bellied sap-sucking dwarf, them's fighting words."

Then Gorilla grabbed for Stinker, and I threw my weight against both of them, so all three of us went crashing down onto a snowy lawn, and the three-way battle royal raged just the way it always had.

"SO HOW WAS WASHINGTON?" Kris asked.

We were standing in her huge living room. It was the first time we had been alone in more than a month. She was wearing tight white pants and a red silk shirt that showed off her figure to perfection. "Good," I told her. "I found out a lot about my father."

"Yeah, you seem better now," she said. "You were pretty crazed last time we talked . . . when we had that fight."

"It wasn't a fight, just an argument," I told her. I couldn't keep my eyes off the way her silk shirt swelled out from the dip of her shoulders to cover the twin peaks of her breasts. I knew she could feel my gaze, but I couldn't stop. "How've things been going with you?"

"Good," she said. "I drove down to Colgate with

my mom and looked around. I really liked it. If I get in, I think I'm gonna go there."

"You'll get in," I told her, patting her affectionately on the shoulder. I let my hand stay there and slid it slowly down her back.

She looked at me and moved away half a step. "I don't know," she said. "Their admission standards are pretty high."

"Well, I think you're pretty bright," I told her honestly. "You saw things about me that I didn't see myself. Maybe you should be a psychology major."

"I can promise you one thing. I won't be a chemistry major," she said.

"Would you like to go upstairs . . . for a back rub?" I asked her. "Come on. I think I could make you feel terrific today."

She shook her head. "No, thanks," she said. "I don't feel stiff today."

"I do," I told her. I stepped in close and put my arms around the small of her back and hugged her to me so that her feet came off the floor.

She hugged me back for a minute and then said, "Ron, we'd better talk."

I set her down. "I thought that's what we've been doing."

She walked over to the couch and sat down. I followed her. She didn't say anything for a while. She just looked at me.

"Kris, I've changed a bit," I said. "I . . . think I can bend my own rules a little more now. Not that I'm a wild man or anything, but I'm trying to be more open and tolerant of other people. My father had a

165

thing about not judging other people or their ideas too harshly, and I'm trying to follow his advice."

She didn't say anything.

"I'm not saying I'm gonna become an alcoholic or a drug user, but I think the two of us could have a good time together now. I'd like to try."

She shook her head.

"Why not?"

"Ron, I value your friendship," she said. "I really do. And sometime in the future when you unbend a little more, I'd love to get drunk with you and see what you're like. And I'd like to beat you at bowling. But I don't think we should go out anymore."

"Why?" I asked. "During the time I was . . . brooding . . . I alienated a lot of my friends. Stinker, Coach Brogan, and even Gorilla a little bit. But we've all gone back to the way it was." My voice became more urgent. "Kris, I'm really sorry I didn't return your phone calls for a while, but I was going through a tough time."

She smiled a sad smile. "Going out with a girl isn't the same as being friends with a guy," she said. "There are other things involved. Of course your friends took you back, and I want to stay friends, too. But that's all I want."

I looked at her. Her long blonde hair was tied in a ponytail. Her big blue eyes were warm, and they sparkled. "I don't understand you," I told her.

Then she spoke fast and a little more loudly. "We were supposed to be going out. Maybe you had your problems, but for weeks I waited for you to come over or for the phone to ring or for a letter or . . . something. And nothing came. I waited day by day and hour by hour. I really liked you, but nothing came and I got tired of waiting. And a little angry. And then I started getting letters from Tommy Faye."

My whole body tensed up when she spoke her former boyfriend's name.

Kris's voice took on a new tone of serious determination. "You know, we'd been going out for two years before we decided to break up because he was going off to college. I missed him a lot, and it turns out that he was missing me too. He'll be back soon for a vacation and he's also planning to spend the summer in town, and he wants to try to keep it going between us." She paused and looked right at me, and I admired her courage even as I dreaded what she was about to say. "I've thought about it a lot, and I've decided that I'd like to try to keep it going with him."

"Maybe if I had returned some of your phone calls you wouldn't feel this way? I didn't give you much of a choice."

She shrugged her shoulders. "I like you very much," she said, "but I think you and I should just be good friends. In the long run, I think it will be better for both of us. Okay?"

She had never looked lovelier to me than she did at that moment. Her small, delicate chin was upturned, and her moist lips were taut with contradictory feelings of firm resolve and sympathy. I could see that she had made a very definite decision.

"Please," she said. "Ron, okay?"

I breathed out, and my lungs felt like a balloon slowly deflating. "Okay," I finally agreed.

I KNEW SOMETHING odd was coming.

Coach Brogan had so much respect for the importance of a good education and the necessity of doing well in school that he never yanked one of his wrestlers out of class for any reason. In my three years in the high school wrestling program, I had never heard of it happening. So when a guy from the phys ed office walked into my biology class, handed Mr. Fitch a note, and nodded for me to follow him, I knew something unusual was happening.

"What's up?" I asked him in the hallway.

"I don't know," he said. "Coach Brogan wants to see you. Immediately."

He turned into the gymnasium, and I walked to the phys ed office alone. The door was closed. I knocked, and Coach Brogan's voice called, "Come in." I walked into the room and was surprised to see Coach Brogan sitting at his desk and Carl Stoner sitting in a chair across from him. "Close the door and sit down," Coach Brogan said.

I sat down in a chair next to Carl. He was sitting on the edge of his chair and kept rubbing his fist nervously into his palm. He looked at me once and then looked away.

"Carl came to see me today," Coach Brogan said. "He has something to say to you, Ron."

I waited. Carl Stoner didn't seem like he had anything to say to anybody. He was staring down at the stone floor.

The room looked the same as it always had; it was cluttered with sports equipment and trophies and sweat suits. Coach Brogan, however, seemed unusually excited. His eyes shot keen lasers at Carl, who still hadn't uttered a sound.

"I did it," Carl finally muttered.

"What?" I asked him.

He glanced at me, and his eyes were redder and more feverish than they had been at wrestling practice. I could tell that something frightening was going on inside of him. "What do you think?" he asked.

I shrugged, but deep down I began to feel a vague suspicion.

"Start at the beginning, Carl," Coach Brogan prompted him.

Carl looked at him and then at the wrestling trophies in the case behind him and finally back at me. "I really hate your guts," he said to me. "You know that?"

I nodded. "Yeah," I said.

"So a week before the first wrestling practice, I was at a party and I smoked some pot. Then at practice Coach Brogan announced the drug test and I got scared. I figured I might test positive even though a week had gone by, but I didn't know what I could do to get out of it."

I still wasn't sure exactly what was coming, but I had a sense that it was the answer to a huge riddle. I watched him closely. He had large bags under his eyes, and his right hand, which rested on his knee, shook slightly.

"I went down and was one of the first guys to take the test. Afterward I went out and hung around with the rest of the team, but I kept getting more and more worried. I guess I knew I was going to fail, and I didn't know what they'd do to me or if everyone would find out. I figured I wouldn't be able to wrestle this season. Then the fire bell rang."

I thought back to that morning and how there had been a small fire in one of the chem labs that had set off the smoke alarm. I remembered the school emptying out and how I had talked to Kris and set up our bowling date.

Carl plunged forward. "I started out with the rest of the crowd and then I stopped. I didn't know why myself, but I suddenly turned around and headed back into the nurse's office. Everyone was gone. I walked to the inner office, and the urine samples from our team were sitting on a table with numbered stickers on them and a coding sheet next to them. The guy from the testing agency must have gone out with everyone else."

Carl was looking right at me. His eyes blazed as he continued. "I suddenly knew what I was going to do. I found the number on my test tube. I could have switched it with anyone on the team. I figured if they failed they'd just take a retest and go on wrestling. But I took the time to find your tube and change the sticker with my own."

There didn't seem to be enough air in the room. I could feel my breaths getting bigger and my blood getting hotter. I tried to control myself.

"We had just had that fight in practice," he said. "And anyway, I thought it would be funny if Mr. Big Shot, Captain, Eagle Scout, Straight-A Student, Ron 'I'm better than you are' Woods got taken down a few notches. So I switched the numbered stickers and hurried out of there, and nobody saw me.

"When I heard you decided not to take the retest, I didn't know what to do. If I told you or Coach Brogan, I would be off the team. And I didn't feel I owed you anything, so I decided to let you wreck things for yourself. What did I care? I figured I could even take your spot."

"So why are you telling me now?" I asked him. "You got away with it."

He got out of his chair, and when he talked it sounded like he was angrier at himself than he had ever been at me. "I couldn't sleep," he said. "I tried everything. Pills. A couple of shots before bed. Outdoor exercise. Warm milk. Hot baths. If I was lucky, I would get one or two hours a night. It's been like that all season. Last night after you tried to help me out in wrestling practice, I didn't get any sleep at all. Not

171

even a minute. That was it. I just can't take it anymore. So now you know."

Carl headed for the door.

"As of this moment, you're off the wrestling team,"
Coach Brogan said to him. Then he turned to me and
said, "Ron, whatever his reasons were, it took a lot of
courage for Carl to come in and tell me this today."

"If you're gonna suggest we shake hands, make up,
and be friends, you can forget it," Carl Stoner said. "I
still hate his guts."

"I'm not crazy about your guts either," I told him.
"You bastard!"

Carl Stoner gave us both one last look. "I'm goin'
home to sleep," he muttered as he turned the knob
and yanked the door open. "If I can't sleep now, I'll
go nuts."

Then he was gone, and Coach Brogan was looking
at me across his desk.

"So that's what happened," I said.

"I never doubted that you didn't use drugs," Coach
Brogan said. "But who could ever have figured that
one out?"

"So what do we do now?" I asked him.

He grinned. "Do you feel like wrestling? As your
coach, I can now certify that you passed a drug test.
Your real sample tested fine. I'll have to clear it with
the county board, but there shouldn't be a problem
once they hear what happened."

"Then I would still be allowing a drug test to decide my fate," I said. "Although I did agree to take
the first test, so maybe I should just make the most of
this—unexpected news."

172

Coach Brogan got out of his chair and walked out from behind his desk. He stood above me. His biceps bunched into mounds of muscle, and his fingers folded into huge fists. "Let me make this one easy for you, Ron," he said, and he was half smiling. "You said you wouldn't take a retest, and you didn't. You said you never used drugs in your life, and time has proved you right. You made a tough moral stand, and I admire the heck out of you for it." He took a step closer to me. "But if you still decide you don't want to wrestle, I'm going to wrap your tonsils around your toes."

I looked up at him, and I had to smile a little bit. "When you put it that way," I said, "what can I say? Do you have a sweat suit I can borrow?"

THE ROAD BACK was long and hard. I was in superb shape from all my workouts in the basement, but
being in shape does not make you ready to wrestle. I
hadn't tied up with an opponent on the mats in
months, and all of my skills were dulled. The first time
I actually wrestled someone during one of our team
practices, it felt like I was wrestling underwater. My
reactions were slow. I couldn't anticipate my opponent's movement the way I used to. My balance was
off, and several times I felt awkward just moving
around the mat. After the match, I could feel the freshmen wrestlers looking at me and wondering if this was
the fearsome Ron Woods they had heard so much
about.

My first varsity match was against Lincoln High. I
wrestled a new kid named Firsch who had bad acne

and very little wrestling ability. I managed to pin him in the third period, but I had no illusions that I had returned to form. It had been a sloppy performance, and I had been lucky rather than good.

"You're not that far away," Coach Brogan reassured me. He had me wrestle a lot of extra matches during practice, and my moves and timing slowly improved. Coach Brogan was eating over at my house two or three times a week now. At first it was a little strange seeing him at wrestling practice and then seeing him at my house later that night. After a while the strangeness wore off, and I got used to his presence at our dinner table. It was kind of fun to have him around.

My second match was against Doug Randall at Fairfield High School. I almost lost. Doug was a senior and a good wrestler, and halfway through the second period he wrapped his legs around my back in a figure four and broke me down to the mat. He went for a half nelson, slipping his right arm under my right arm and around the back of my head, and then tried to use the figure four along with the half nelson to turn me over onto my back in a dangerous pinning combination. As he turned me, he had to loosen up slightly with his figure four, and I was able to battle my way out, but it was a very close call. I won the match on points.

Gorilla and Stinker were a big help. It was great to be back with them, joking and fooling around. "You're holding back—not being aggressive enough," Gorilla said, and I knew he was right. I still didn't have enough confidence to keep the pressure on with take-down tries and pinning combinations.

175

Gorilla was still going out with Mary Renardi, so Stinker and I spent a lot of time as a twosome. One Sunday we went to the Paramus Park Mall and spent three or four hours scoping out women. The high point of the day came when Stinker spotted an absolute goddess floating along in a miniskirt. She had the longest, loveliest legs imaginable, and Stinker trailed her from one end of the mall to the other, trying to think of something to say. I trailed Stinker and waited to see what he would come up with. Finally he got on the escalator about ten feet above her and began to walk down. I watched. He reached her, tapped her on her shoulder, and asked her for the time. I saw her check her watch. Then Stinker said something else to her, and I saw her smile. They talked a few seconds more, and then the escalator reached the floor level and she stepped off, but Stinker's attention had been so riveted on her that he wasn't prepared. He tried to step off and was kind of thrown off at the same second, and he ended up tripping over his feet and falling flat on his back. The goddess giggled and walked away, and I had to hold my stomach so it wouldn't come off as I rocked back and forth with laughter. Good old Stinker.

The low point of the day came when I spotted Kris walking hand in hand with Tommy Faye, her old boyfriend. He must have come back on his winter vacation. They looked very natural together. He held her hand loosely, as if he knew she wouldn't stray far from him. When he said something and smiled, she laughed. I ducked behind a pillar and let them walk away without seeing me. It made my whole body feel cold and empty to see her with another guy. I wanted to slug

176

him. But Kris had made her decision, and the only thing I could do was to laugh and joke and whoop it up with Stinker and wait for this cold feeling to pass.

A strange thing happened during our second-to-last match of the year. We were wrestling against Indian Lake High School. They had a very talented wrestler named Jerry Nathan, who fought in my weight class. I had come up against him last year in an early round of the county tournament, and it had taken all my strength and skill to beat him. This year I knew he had a fine record and would be tough.

"You got an unusual fan," Gorilla told me as the 112-pounders circled on the mat. I looked where he was pointing and was amazed to see Igor climbing the bleachers. He sat by himself, watching. When my turn came to wrestle and I walked out on the mat, I couldn't help throwing one quick glance at him. His hard, muscular body rose straight off the bleacher like an outcropping of rock, and his intense eyes followed my every move.

It was a fierce match. Jerry Nathan threw everything he had at me in a dazzling show of wrestling technique. I escaped and reversed and hung on as best I could and finally felt him wearing down. I was a little bit stronger, and by the third period he had stopped attacking and was beginning to wrestle defensively. I knew I was behind on points, so I went for a pin using a combination called the stack. I started with a crotch ride and worked my way into a modified stack position. Jerry resisted as best he could, but I could hear the depth and tiredness of his gasps for breath. Finally I succeeded in grabbing his neck with my left hand and

177

stacking him into a position where he was on his back too cramped to bridge his shoulders off the mat. For seconds he somehow managed to keep one shoulder blade up. I knew I was behind and that the match was almost over, so when the ref finally slapped the mat, announcing the pin, I felt a surge of relief mixed with the thrill of victory.

As the ref held up my hand, I saw Igor stride down the bleachers and head out the exit. He had come only to see one match, and he had seen it.

Right after our school's victory over Indian Lake High School, Coach Brogan filed an appeal to try to make me eligible for the county tournament. Normally, in order to wrestle in the county tournament you need to have at least ten varsity wins that season. Since I had sat out for so long, I had far less than the required number of victories. I was undefeated, however, and since I had been a county runner-up last year and had been kind of victimized by the drug-test-sample switch, Coach Brogan thought there was a good chance that they would let me into the county tournament.

Bob Jenkins came to our school one morning to discuss the appeal. I remembered him from my hearing before the county athletic officers. His bald head glinted under the fluorescent ceiling lights as he read the appeal statement that Coach Brogan had typed up. Every so often he pulled a handkerchief out of his pocket, blew on the lenses of his black-rimmed eyeglasses, and polished them.

We were in the teachers' conference room. I sat next to Coach Brogan, trying not to look nervous. A

178

lot of time and work depended on Bob Jenkins' answer.

Finally he looked up. "I'm sorry," he said. "The
rules are very clear. Ten varsity victories are needed to
enter the county tournament. Ron has only five. He is
therefore ineligible."

"Didn't you read that appeal?" Coach Brogan demanded. "It wasn't Ron's fault he didn't get enough
matches. He was a victim of a cruel and intentional
deception by another member of the team. You can't
hold that against him."

Bob Jenkins stood up. "I sympathize, but the rules
are the rules. In the past we've had appeals from talented wrestlers who have missed large chunks of the
season because of injuries. We have established a firm
policy of turning down such appeals. We just don't
make exceptions."

Coach Brogan stood up to face him. He looked really angry, and Bob Jenkins slid back half a step. "I demand that you bring this appeal before the other members of the county board."

"I have full authority to decide an appeal like this
on my own," Bob Jenkins told him. He looked at me.
"I'm sorry, but my decision is final. I hope you understand the reasons."

I was having trouble believing that it was all going
to come to an end like this. I didn't want to explode
and get all emotional, so I aimed three short words at
him, and they came off my tongue like bazooka shells:
"Just get out."

Bob Jenkins turned on his heel and left. Coach Brogan walked over. "I don't know how to fight this," he said.

"The rules are the rules," I told him. "I guess I was just jinxed this season. Igor probably would have stomped me anyway."

"Probably," he agreed. Then he added, "But not definitely. I can't believe they're not going to let you come to the county tournament."

I took a few deep breaths. "I'm gonna come," I told him. "I'm captain of this team. They may not let me wrestle, but I'm gonna suit up with the guys and stand on the side and yell my tongue out for Gorilla and Stinker and all the other guys who made it into the county tournament. They can't keep me out of the room."

"No," Coach Brogan admitted, "they can't." Then he said, "You've grown up so much these past few months it's . . . remarkable."

"It's been a tough season," I told him. "On and off the mats."

"I respect the way you're handling this," he said. "It's an honor to coach you."

I could see that he had something else he really wanted to say. I waited, and finally I asked him. "Is there something else?"

He opened his mouth and closed it and then opened it again. When his voice came out, it was a whisper from the very center of the man. "I want you to know that I love your mother," he said. "And you too. I guess what I'm trying to say is that it's an honor to know two such wonderful people. And to become

180

involved in your family. You know, I've never had a son."

I didn't know what to say back so I just kind of nodded, and he grinned, and not wrestling in the county tournament suddenly didn't seem such a tragedy.

THE COUNTY CHAMPIONSHIPS were held in the large gymnasium of Fairview College. The bleachers rose up from the gym floor like wooden mountains, their steadily ascending, polished slopes gleaming beneath the huge ceiling lamps. The mats were brand-new, and the referees were the very best in the county. There were always more than a thousand spectators in the stands, and more drifted in as the tournament wore on.

Our team had placed four wrestlers in the tournament this year. Gorilla had had only one loss all season and was one of the tournament favorites. Stinker had made it with an eleven-win and seven-loss record. A junior named Anderson had improved a lot during the course of the year and finished with three straight upsets to qualify. And a tough sophomore, Hernandez, had surprised everyone by battling his way to a ten-

and-eight record and a qualifying berth. Some of our best wrestlers hadn't qualified, and we didn't really have a shot at the team title, which is decided on the basis of which team scores the most points in the tournament. But our whole team was there, all suited up and ready to yell support for Gorilla, Stinker, Anderson, and Hernandez.

The tournament takes place over three days. The first two days, each wrestler fights two single-elimination matches. The semifinals, runner-up matches, and finals are on the third day.

Hernandez, at 112 pounds, was our first team member to wrestle. I thought that since he was only a sophomore, Hernandez might panic and lose quickly, but he showed a lot of poise. He got into trouble early when his more experienced opponent put him into a nasty hold called the grapevine. Hernandez managed to avoid being pinned, but when the first period ended, he was way behind on points. In the second period he was quickly broken down again, but after a few minutes he came up with a neat reversal, using a whizzer and a knee spin to turn things around. Finally, in the third period he came on strong and took the close match on points. He was strong and well conditioned for a sophomore, and although his technique wasn't polished, he was a tough kid with a good idea of the basics.

Anderson lost his first match at 127 pounds. He came up against one of the best wrestlers in the county and did well to escape being pinned. So now we were down to only three wrestlers. I could feel my excitement level rising as Stinker's turn got nearer and nearer. A lot of wrestlers from other schools came up to me and told me they'd heard about what had happened and they felt bad for me. They said they wished I was in the tournament. I had never even met some of them before, and their sympathy made me feel a little better about not being able to wrestle. It was especially hard because I knew I was in tournament shape, and I had to watch a number of so-so wrestlers fight and lose while I sat in the bleachers or stood on the sideline.

"Good luck, Stinker," I told him. "You can do it, man."

He gets real tense before big matches. "Gonna give it my best shot," he muttered. Then he was on the mat shaking hands with his opponent while Gorilla and Coach Brogan and I stood shoulder to shoulder, watching and waiting to yell. Stinker was never a great wrestler, but he understood the sport and had a few pet combinations that he could do quite well. He was fighting a talented freshman with lots of strength and guts but very little experience. For the first period they circled and tied up and circled and tied up, and neither was able to get a clear advantage. Halfway into the second period, Stinker maneuvered his way into a cross-body ride and began putting on all sorts of pressure. Gorilla and I hollered for a pin, and Coach Brogan was punching the air with excitement. Stinker didn't get the pin, but he did get lots of points and managed to hold off the freshman during the third period for a fairly easy decision. I really respected Gorilla for shouting for Stinker and giving off so much energy when he had his own first match to worry about. But that's Gorilla—he thinks of everyone else but himself.

I was in the bleachers for Igor's first match. It was over with lightning speed. His opponent, a sophomore, was clearly outclassed, outmuscled, and scared of him. Igor had him on his back in little more than a minute and then clamped his shoulders down for the fall in another ten seconds. Once Igor has a wrestler on his back, he gets the pin more quickly than any other wrestler I have ever seen. It's almost impossible to resist his combination of strength and fury.

Our team sat together at a table in the cafeteria during lunch, and Hernandez got a lot of free advice. He was going up against a former county champion in his afternoon match, and everyone knew he would lose, but there was something about his rugged face and flashing black eyes that convinced us he would fight his heart out.

"Forget who he is and just go after him," I advised him before the match.

"Yeah, keep the pressure on. Don't let him dictate the fight," Coach Brogan told him. "And watch out for the chicken wing combined with a half nelson. It's his favorite pinning combo. Don't let him tie your arms up."

Hernandez fought through the first period dead even, and his courage won over a lot of the crowd. But in the second period his opponent broke him to the mat with a head drive and then slid his left arm in for a chicken wing. I knew Hernandez was in trouble. He knew it too and tried everything to escape, but when his opponent switched his weight over to the other side of Hernandez' body and applied a half nel-

185

son, both of Hernandez' arms were tied up. He struggled and flailed, but the former county champ used his holds to force Hernandez over onto his back, threw his right leg out for balance, and kept increasing the pressure until the ref finally slapped the mat, announcing the pin. The crowd gave Hernandez a big cheer, and he deserved it; I looked forward to seeing what he would do in the tournament next year.

"You got to win this one for me, Stinker," I told him as he got ready. "All I can do this tournament is cheer, and I've only got two wrestlers left to cheer for."

"Don't worry about this guy," Stinker told me. "I've fought him before, and I know how to beat him."

Stinker's a smart wrestler, and I believed him. "Just don't get careless," I cautioned him.

It was a war. I began to go hoarse by the start of the third period, with the scores dead even and both wrestlers giving everything they had. It ended dead even too, and since there was no big difference in riding time, the ref and the judges decided the match. I watched Stinker nervously waiting in the center of the mat, and I held my breath. Then the ref raised Stinker's hand and his face lit up, and Gorilla and I charged out onto the mat to congratulate him.

Gorilla swamped his opponent. It was nice to see all those years of learning and conditioning pay off for my big friend, even though I couldn't help wishing they were also paying off for me. He was stronger, faster, and had lots more wrestling smarts than the guy they

186

put him up against, and he coasted to a major decision without ever really being in any danger.

We spent that evening planning. My two best friends were the only wrestlers from our team left in the tournament. I felt bad about not being there with them, but it took my mind off my disappointment to share their excitement and go over their next day's matches. We met at Gorilla's house. We played a little Ping-Pong down in the basement and then sat together and held kind of a strategy session.

Strategy can be very important in fighting a match the right way. For example, Stinker was going to fight a tall wrestler in his first match the next day. Tall wrestlers have good leverage, but they tend to overextend themselves. We advised Stinker to try to grab an exposed arm or wrist and then move into him quickly for a double-leg attack. We also had all seen this guy wrestle several times, and we tried to remember his favorite takedowns and pinning combinations. We did the same for Gorilla's opponents, even though I'm not sure he needed our help.

The second day of the tournament there were fewer wrestlers and more fans. Stinker was so tense he didn't want to talk to Gorilla or me and walked off by himself. Gorilla appeared perfectly relaxed—he never lets the pressure get to him.

"C'mon, Stinker. C'mon," we yelled to him as his match started. His opponent was tall but not at all awkward, and I knew my buddy was in for a tough fight. Stinker tried to follow the strategy that we had talked about, but his tall opponent was unexpectedly quick and used his leverage to great advantage. In the second period he locked an arm bar on Stinker's right arm, and then spent long minutes trying to pry Stinker over onto his back by stepping over him and circling to the front. Stinker resisted well, but he lost a lot of points and energy. He fought back courageously in the third period, and even pulled off a neat switch for a reversal, but he just couldn't generate enough pressure. I was hoarse by the time the last second clicked off the clock, and Coach Brogan was punching the air with excitement and frustration. Stinker got a nice cheer from the crowd for his efforts, and he didn't seem too upset at having been eliminated.

"Hell of a try," I told him.

"Had him scared the whole third period," Gorilla said, clapping him on the back.

Stinker looked at Gorilla. "It's up to you now, big guy. I did my best, but now you're all we got left."

The Gorilla rose to the challenge. He won his third fight on a major decision and came off the mat looking relaxed and very confident. His second match of the day was much closer, and our whole team shouted and worried as Gorilla and his massive opponent tugged away at each other like two huge jungle apes in a death struggle. For a while the outcome was very much in doubt, but Gorilla put together a miraculous takedown move late in the third period for a come-from-behind win. That match took a lot out of him. His huge chest heaved as the breath ripped in and out of his lungs.

At one point during that day I headed into the hall for a drink of water and passed Igor, who was heading out. We both slowed down as we passed each other. I was kind of surprised when he turned his head and growled, "Four matches, four pins, Woods."

I shrugged. "It's easy when you're wrestling stiffs."

The skin tightened over his forehead and cheekbones as he scowled with anger. "It's even easier when you sit out the tournament," he snarled, and then he was gone, and I tried to recover from the sudden surge of energy and fear that I always feel when I meet Igor face to face.

That night Mary Renardi also attended our strategy session. I didn't really know her very well, and I was impressed by how much she obviously cared for Gorilla. She stood behind him as we talked and massaged his shoulders and neck. Every few minutes he would close his huge hands over hers and draw her palms forward for a kiss.

"Don't let the Beach Ball get on top of you" was all the help Stinker and I could give him. Gorilla wrestled in the unlimited weight division, and his semifinal match the next morning would be against a gigantic, fat blob of a wrestler whom everyone called the Beach Ball. The Beach Ball was huge and round and strong and must have outweighed Gorilla by seventy-five or a hundred pounds. For Gorilla to win, he had to keep away for at least a period and tire the Beach Ball out. Once deflated, the huge wrestler could be beaten.

Our whole team showed up the third day to watch the outcome of the tournament and cheer Gorilla on. Stinker and I both suited up to make it feel even more like we were going to be helping our buddy fight. Coach Brogan took Gorilla aside before the match and cautioned him not to fight in close. "Don't go power to power until he's tired himself out. Circle and feint. Make him move around the mat. You'll be able to hear from his breathing when it's safe to move inside."

The audience gave a big cheer for each of the semifinal contestants. Gorilla shook hands with the Beach Ball and then spent the first period following his strategy perfectly. He tied up and managed to look aggressive while staying away from the Beach Ball's strength and power.

He started well in the second period, and even from where I stood I could hear the Beach Ball begin to huff and puff. But about midway through the period the Beach Ball managed to get control and break Gorilla down to the mat, and then the Beach Ball kind of rolled over my friend. Gorilla battled back valiantly. He had always been prodigiously strong, and several times he seemed at the point of escaping as his huge arms pried and lifted and strained at the weight that kept pressing him down toward the mat. But a man can't survive beneath a mountain, and with two minutes to go in the period my best friend Gorilla had his shoulders pinned to the mat.

He looked dejected as he came off the mat, his large frame still shaking with the effort of trying to resist the Beach Ball. I tried to console him, and Stinker and Coach Brogan tried, too, but when Mary Renardi came down and wrapped his sweaty body up in a big, loving hug, we all moved away. She didn't have to say anything to console him, and after a few minutes Gorilla was back with us, looking as relaxed as ever.

"I learned a lot from that match," he told us. "And

190

I think I'll win the afternoon match for third place in the county."

"What did you learn?" Stinker wanted to know.

"I learned that once a crazed walrus gets on top of you, it's all over," he said with a grin. "I mean that guy was *huge*."

Gorilla was true to his word. He won his afternoon match, and we all cheered as Bob Jenkins, the vice-president of the county athletic board, handed him the silver cup for third place. Gorilla held it above his head, and it shimmered brilliantly.

Some of our teammates left after that, but most of us stuck around for the county championship final matches. All of the finalists were superb wrestlers who had survived battles to get there, and there was no sloppy wrestling. Hernandez watched the finals of his weight class with great interest because the guy who beat him was out there gunning for the championship. The guy won, and Hernandez kept shaking his head and saying, "Hell, he was good, but he wasn't *that* good." I knew what he meant—once you've tied up with someone and felt their strengths and weaknesses, you realize that they can be beaten and that you could be champion someday too.

"This should be interesting," Coach Brogan said to me as Igor came out for his final match.

"The boxer versus the slugger," I nodded. "Let's see what Jerry Nathan can do."

The crowd gave Igor a tremendous hand. He was well on his way to getting the Outstanding Wrestler in the Tournament Award. So far he had pinned every single one of his opponents, and none of them had taken him past the second period. He walked out in that curious way of his, so that his feet never seemed to leave the mat. The tan ripples of his muscular body were magnificent in the brightly lit gym, and his bald head gave him an otherworldly quality, as if he were a demon risen from hell to take the county championship.

Even so, I figured it would be a tough match. Jerry Nathan had been very impressive in getting to the finals, and his superb wrestling technique would be very hard for Igor to crack. I remembered my own hard-fought struggle with Jerry and how during the first two periods of our match he had dazzled me with his superb moves and flawless body control.

It was a rout. Igor swept in for a double-leg takedown so quickly it was hard to believe he had started from a nearly still position. Jerry was fast, but Igor's body had flashed in and taken him by surprise, and as he secured both of Jerry's legs, it was as if Jerry had been struck by lightning. Then Igor pulled off a remarkable feat of strength. In one tremendous surge he drove upward with his legs and lifted Jerry clear off the ground, so that he held him high over his right shoulder. The crowd in the gym gasped. Igor reached inside Jerry's crotch to gain control of his hips. According to the high school wrestling rules, to earn takedown points after a lift, you need to establish control of your body by planting both feet and one knee on the mat before bringing your opponent down. Igor planted his feet and knee and brought Jerry down to the mat as lightly as if he had been a rag doll, and somehow Igor had reached around so that as he laid

192

Jerry down, he already had a cradle hold. Jerry bucked and strained, but the ref was kneeling down watching his shoulders and soon slapped the mat to announce the pin. The time of the match was about thirty-five seconds. Igor hadn't even broken a sweat.

The ref held up Igor's hand to announce the pin, and the crowd roared. Bob Jenkins came out with the huge county championship cup and presented it to Igor and shook his hand. The crowd roared again. Igor took it from him and looked at it, and then held it up to the light, and then looked at it again. Then he handed it back to Bob Jenkins.

He tilted his head back so that his windpipe was a straight tunnel from deep within his lungs, and he let out a yell that echoed through the massive gym. *"Woods!"*

I saw his eyes sweeping over the rows of fans till he spotted our team colors and found me. *"Woods!"* he shouted again.

"Has he gone nuts?" Stinker asked me. "What's he want?"

But I didn't answer. I was looking down at Igor, and I suddenly found myself standing up off the bleacher. My own personal monster was summoning me to combat. I tilted my own head back and shouted, *"Igor!"*

"Woods!" he bellowed again, and the whole auditorium was suddenly dead silent as people looked from him to me to him.

"I'm coming," I shouted and started down the bleachers.

And then people started to clap. At first I think it

193

was just my own team members who called out to me, "Get him, Ron. Go. He's callin' you out. C'mon." But as I moved down through the bleachers and people made way for me, the crowd realized what was happening, and the noise level in the gym shot up higher and higher. Wrestling fans are a devoted bunch. They knew me from past tournaments and were aware of my rivalry with Igor, and the papers had had a few articles on why I wasn't in this tournament. So they understood, and as I passed them, people reached out to me and clapped and wished me luck.

Then I was on the floor of the gym, moving toward the mats. I was dimly conscious that Coach Brogan and Gorilla were walking on either side of me and that the rest of the team had filed down, too, and were trailing behind us. But my whole concentration was riveted on Igor, who stood in the dead center of the mat, watching me come. I walked close to him and stopped. His lips parted, and I thought he was going to speak, but he just snarled through clenched teeth.

"Let's fight," I snarled back.

Then Bob Jenkins came between us. "I can't permit this," he said. "The tournament rules are very clear. We can't sanction this match. The county championship has already been decided. The trophy cup has already been awarded."

"I don't care about the trophy cup," I told him.

"Why don't you just get off the mat?" Coach Brogan said to him, and from the way Bob Jenkins flinched, you could tell that he was a little afraid of our coach.

Bob Jenkins turned to the referee. He was Walt

Howard, the best ref in the county. He had wrestled on the U.S. Olympic team at the Mexico Olympics, and even though he was now in middle age, he didn't look like he had put on an ounce of fat. He was a very handsome black man, with a chin that looked like it had been chiseled out of marble, and clear, keen eyes. "Walt," Bob Jenkins said, "the county cannot authorize this fight. As a county official, you can't officiate it."

Walt Howard looked back at Bob Jenkins, and then he looked at Igor and me. "Hell," he said, "I'm gonna ref this fight. If I can't do it here, we'll go out to the parking lot, and I'll ref it out there."

"I won't permit it," Bob Jenkins said. And then I saw Don Schiller, the president of the county board, walk down out of the audience. His silver hair waved as he hurried toward us, and he was smiling. "What's the trouble, Bob?" he asked.

"We can't permit this fight," Bob Jenkins said. "The championship has already been decided. The trophy has been presented. The rules are very definite."

Don Schiller was silent for about five seconds. Then he said, "Screw the rules, Bob. Can't you see these two boys want to wrestle?"

Bob Jenkins looked like he would still argue. He opened his mouth and then closed it again. Then he turned his back on us and walked away.

"Good luck to both of you," Don Schiller said.

Then I was on the side of the mats, peeling off my team sweats and stretching out my arms and legs. The gym was buzzing with sound, and my blood was racing through the highways of my arteries at dizzying speeds.

"He's gonna come right in for the takedown," Coach Brogan told me. "He always does."

"Don't give an inch," Stinker advised. "Power to power."

"Think about that picture under your chin-up bar," Gorilla whispered. "You've fought this fight all winter. Win it."

Then I was out on the mat facing Igor, and I got that jolt of surprise and fear from seeing his eyes focused on me, narrowing with more concentrated fury than seemed possible.

He came in for a double leg, and even though I was expecting it, I barely had time to shoot my legs out and tie up with him. I had forgotten what it was like to fight him. The sour breath. The constantly building pressure. The strength that seemed irresistible. The growling breaths and the pulsing fury.

He backed out and circled and then shot in again when I was in midstep and got one of my legs. He tried to lift me, but I lowered my center of gravity and used my weight to resist the lift. He began circling, still holding my leg, trying to disrupt my balance so that he could get the lift. I countered as best I could, but he managed a dump and spun behind me for control.

That period ticked off terribly slowly as he maintained control and broke me down to the mat time and time again, while I fought off pinning combinations and tried unsuccessfully to escape. His strength and power were tremendous, and his wrestling technique was also superb. There were no weaknesses or letups for me to exploit.

196

I was behind on points when the first period ended, but I had never been in serious danger. "Now take him," Gorilla urged. His always calm face was as excited as I'd ever seen it. "Show him what you can do."

I looked around the gym at the rows and rows of fans. I took a number of deep breaths. I felt fresh and strong—lack of conditioning wouldn't be a problem.

A few minutes into the second period, I broke Igor down to the mat. Even on his stomach, with me in control, he managed to apply pressure. It always felt like he was just a split second away from reversing. I tried all sorts of ways of getting him over onto his back, but he countered brilliantly. And then, with just a few minutes left in the period, I got careless for a second. He was on one knee and I was behind him, searching for a hold. With amazing speed, he did a perfect trap roll, rolling onto his right shoulder and using my arm, which had been gripping him around the waist, to throw me over onto my back. I tried to whirl sideways, but he was on me instantly, straining for the pin.

Then began a nightmare period that could only have been two minutes long but seemed to go on forever. There I was once again on my back in the center of the mat at the county tournament with Igor on top, pressuring for the pin with all the strength of a desperate maniac. I bridged and arched, thrashed and turned, using every bit of strength I had to keep both my shoulder blades from touching the mat at the same moment. Several times I expected to hear the ref slap the mat for the pin, but I never gave up and each time managed to somehow keep one of my shoulder blades up. The pressure never let up. The sour breath invaded my head and began to weaken my resistance. The growls were savage. Just when I was about to give up, the whistle blew, announcing the end of the period. The crowd cheered my miraculous survival.

Gorilla and Stinker and the rest of the team left me alone during the break. Coach Brogan only asked me, "You're way behind on points. Do you know what you have to do?"

I nodded. I was thinking of the long winter of sleepless nights and workouts in my basement, of loneliness and self-imposed isolation. I thought about my father and the picture that now hung on my wall above my bed. If he had been alive, he would have been here, sitting in the front row of bleachers. I sort of felt his presence, and I was also conscious of Coach Brogan pacing behind me, wanting to give me advice but not wanting to break in on my concentration.

The third and final period was wild. Igor wasn't tired at all, and neither was I. We tied up and broke off, tried takedowns and countered. Somewhere in my stomach I could feel each second tick off the clock. And then, as we were circling, I grabbed Igor's right arm in an arm drag and pulled him around, knocking his leg support out from under him with my own right leg. I pivoted toward him on the mat and slid into a control position.

My best pinning combination has always been the cross face to a double armlock. They also call this pinning combination the butcher, because your opponent ends up on his back with both of his arms helplessly circled by your left arm, so that he looks like a steer

198

tied up for the slaughter. I got the necessary cross face and snagged Igor's right ankle with my right hand, and then I pulled his body toward me. Somehow he resisted. I pulled harder. Still nothing. I gave one last tremendous pull, and he budged and then lost it completely as I pulled him onto his back. And then I started to pile up the points.

It was like trying to pin a curved piece of iron. When he went into his back bridge, his arch and balance were perfect. When he tried to turn or roll to shake me off, it was all I could do to hang on. But I had been wrestling for a long time and was in superb shape, and I wasn't going to let him off the hook. Several times I was sure I had the pin. When the ref blew his whistle to signal the end of the match, I knew I had piled up a lot of points. Igor and I both glanced up at the scoreboard simultaneously. The score was fifteen to fifteen. The riding times gave neither of us an advantage. The match would be decided by the judges and the ref.

I stood there waiting. I guess Coach Brogan and Gorilla and Stinker were yelling and the crowd was making noise too, but I didn't hear anything. I was just frozen still in time, waiting for the decision. Igor stood a few feet away, motionless and unblinking, as if he had been hypnotized.

Walt Howard came onto the mat and held our two hands down for a long second. I looked at the mat. There were streaks of sweat. My heart had stopped beating and my brain had stopped thinking, and the only part of my body that was still functioning was my eyes, which looked down at the streaks of sweat on the gray wrestling mat. Then Walt Howard raised my hand in victory.

Suddenly I returned to reality. The crowd let out a roar that shook the air. Gorilla and Stinker ran onto the mat, and Coach Brogan was right behind them. Gorilla lifted me into the air and passed me to Coach Brogan, who hugged me and set me down.

And that was when Igor snapped. He had been standing in exactly the same spot ever since Walt Howard had announced the decision by raising my hand. Suddenly he came back to life. He charged me, sweeping people aside as he came on.

I saw him coming and braced for it, but Walt Howard got him by one arm and Coach Brogan got him by the other, and they slowed him down. Yet even with these two powerful men trying to restrain him, Igor still found a way to surge forward. His eyes were narrow with fury, and his breath came in gasping, growling heaves as he fought his way toward me.

A couple of people grabbed me to keep me away, but I found myself dragging them toward him. I inched closer and he inched closer till we stared at each other face to face. His pupils had shrunk to needlepoints of sharp hatred, and when he spoke, his guttural growl vibrated with rage. "I beat you. You're nothing. You're afraid of me. I'll fight you again. *I'll destroy you!*"

I leaned even closer, so that our eyes were only inches apart. I looked right down into the essence of his hatred, and I said in sharp, clear words, "Die, monster, die."

ABOUT THE AUTHOR

DAVID KLASS is the author of three other young adult novels: *Breakaway Run, A Different Season,* and *The Atami Dragons.* He notes, "My challenge in writing this book was to make it clear why Ron is willing to take such a public stand at this particular moment in his life, and to show how the issues of honor, fear, guilt, and duty become interwoven."

Mr. Klass, a Yale graduate, is presently studying filmmaking. He lives in Los Angeles, California.